CHEER USA!

GO, GIRL, GO!

By Jeanne Betancourt

AN
APPLE
PAPERBACK

SCHOLASTIC INC.
New York Toronto London Auckland Sydney
Mexico City New Delhi Hong Kong

For Carole Halpin

Thank you to Janine Santamauro Knight, Head
Cheerleading Coach for St. Joseph by the Sea.

Cover illustration by Karen Hudson

ISBN 0-590-97806-3

12 11 10 9 8 7 6 5 4   9/9 1 2 3 4/0

Printed in the U.S.A.   40

First Scholastic printing, October 1998

Emily Granger jumped out of bed, stuck out her arms, and twirled around like a ceiling fan. The first day of middle school was finally here! She was finally starting seventh grade. Denim shorts and a green tank top hung over her desk chair. New sandals stuck out from under the chair. School supplies were neatly piled on the desk next to a purple backpack. Emily ran into the hall. If she hurried, she could beat her sister Lynn to the bathroom.

Returning from the bathroom a few minutes later, Emily met Lynn in the hall.

"Slow down," Lynn said in a groggy voice. "Where's the fire?"

"It's the first day of school!" exclaimed Emily as she rushed past to her room. Lynn isn't one bit excited, thought Emily. Maybe the first day of eleventh grade wasn't as big a deal as the first day of seventh grade in a *whole new school*.

The phone was ringing when Emily came into her room. She picked it up on the second ring. "Hi, Alexis," she said into the receiver.

"Ah, excuse me," said a surprised man's voice on the other end. "I must have the wrong number."

"Sorry," said Emily, "I thought it was my friend. Who is it you were calling?"

1

"The Manor Hotel," the man answered.

Emily felt herself blush. Just because Alexis said she'd call her before school didn't mean anyone who called would be Alexis. Especially when your family runs a hotel and lives there.

"This is The Manor Hotel," said Emily, "but you have the wrong extension. You want 555-3000. That's the front desk."

As soon as she put the phone down it rang again. "The Manor Hotel," Emily said into the receiver.

"Emily, it's me, Alexis," said the voice on the other end.

"Are you at your dad's yet?" asked Emily.

"I'm still at my mother's," said Alexis. "I'm dressed, and all my stuff is ready. But Mom is taking forever, and she has to bring me and my stuff to Dad's before I can meet you."

"But we'll still meet in front of that juice place at 8:15, right?"

"Squeeze," said Alexis.

"Right," said Emily.

Emily flipped through the blank pages of her new notebook while she talked to Alexis. She always loved the first day of school. It was so much fun to see everybody after the long summer and get off to a fresh start. Seventh grade in a new school would be even better.

Three elementary schools fed into Claymore

Middle School. Emily's parents and her older sister and brother had all gone to CMS. Her mother and sister had been CMS cheerleaders, and her father and brother had been CMS football and basketball players. And best of all, the Grangers always had the Bulldog mascot — a real brown-and-white bulldog. That tradition had started when her father was a boy. The current Bulldog bulldog was Bubba IV, the great-grandson of Bubba I. For Emily, going to CMS was the continuation of a great family tradition.

"I'm so nervous, Emily," Alexis was saying. "I hardly know anyone in the upper grades. And that school is so big."

"We know lots of people," Emily reassured her. "It'll be great, you'll see. We're finally going to be in seventh grade, Alexis! Today! In an *hour*! And we're going out for cheerleading. That's the best."

"Are you still wearing your shorts?" asked Alexis.

"Yes," answered Emily. "And you're wearing that black miniskirt?"

"Uh-huh," Alexis said.

"Then we're all set," Emily told her. "Meet you at Squeeze at 8:15."

As Emily said good-bye to Alexis, her four-year-old sister, Lily, and Bubba burst into the room. Bubba ran circles around Emily until she

3

bent down and gave him a good-morning hug. Lily climbed up on the bed and plopped down next to Emily's cat, Tiger. While Emily got ready for school, Lily played with Tiger and talked nonstop. Bubba sat in the doorway so he could keep an eye on Emily and Lily and, at the same time, check out any action in the hallway. If Lynn or Edward, Emily's ten-year-old brother, came out of their rooms, Bubba would have to choose which Granger he was going to follow. He'd probably charge up and down the hall three or four times before making up his mind. It was dangerous to walk in the hallway when Bubba was making a big decision like that.

Emily checked herself out in the mirror and grinned happily. She was ready for the first day of school.

"Come on," she told Lily. "Let's go get breakfast."

HARBOR ROAD 7:40 A.M.

Alexis Lewis looked around her mother's empty kitchen. At Emily's house, Alexis thought, there would be a whole bunch of people in the kitchen. Alexis wished she had a big family like Emily. It's always either me and my mother or me and my father, she thought sadly. Her parents had been divorced for so long she could hardly

4

remember living with both of them at the same time.

"Did you eat your breakfast?" Alexis's mother yelled from her upstairs bedroom.

"Yes," Alexis shouted back. "And I'm ready. My bag is at the door. Please hurry, Mom."

Changeover day. Alexis hated it. But at least her father's apartment was close to Emily's house. And her father let her hang out at the Grangers' more than her mother did. He'd even let her sleep over at the Grangers' on a school night.

Alexis dropped her suitcase and green backpack on the kitchen porch and sat on the top step. She wondered if she should have bought a red backpack instead of a green one. And what about her shoes? Did they look okay with the skirt? Alexis felt tired and sick to her stomach. She'd been awake for hours during the night, nervous and excited about starting middle school. When she did fall asleep, she had nightmares about being lost in the new school. In one nightmare, kids laughed at her and kept giving her the wrong directions to her classes. Alexis wished that her elementary school had a seventh and eighth grade, too. She knew practically everybody in her grade at Claymore Elementary School. She'd been captain of the girls' basketball team and editor of the school paper — and never got lost in the hallways.

Alexis burped. The taste of the cereal she'd eaten for breakfast rose to her mouth. What if she threw up at school? Right in the hallway. With everyone watching.

Alexis's mother finally came outside, and they headed for the car. "Big day for you," she said.

"Yeah," said Alexis.

She didn't bother to tell her mother how nervous she felt. Her mother never seemed to be afraid of anything. Alexis wondered if that was because her mother was an emergency room nurse. Or maybe her mother was an emergency room nurse because nothing scared her. Alexis knew that her mother would never have been nervous about going to a new school, let alone throw up because of it.

Irene Lewis started the car and backed out of the driveway. "When are you and Emily trying out for cheerleading?" she asked.

"I don't know," Alexis said. "Maybe they'll tell us today."

"Cheerleading would be fun," her mother said.

"I'm not very good," Alexis mumbled.

"I'm sure you could be," Irene Lewis assured her daughter. "How many times do I have to tell you, honey? You can do anything you want. You just have to want it bad enough. You really want to be a cheerleader, don't you?"

"Of course, I do," answered Alexis. "Emily is doing it, and we practiced all summer. Her sister Lynn helped us, remember? And she's the best cheerleader."

"Good," said her mother. She stopped for a red light. Alexis looked at her watch. If she was late, she hoped Emily would wait for her.

She'd die if she had to go into that school alone.

DELHAVEN DRIVE 8:00 A.M.

Joan Russo-Chazen looked out her bedroom window. A school bus drove by. Was it going to Claymore Middle School? Joan turned and smiled at her reflection in the mirror. Well, *she* was going to Claymore Middle School! CMS! For three years Joan had attended Spencer Day School in Fort Myers. Spencer was an okay school, but none of her classmates lived in Claymore. Joan had no friends her own age in the town she had lived in for three years! She was glad that Spencer stopped at sixth grade, so she had to go to a public school.

Joan took her brown hair out of the ponytail and shook it loose. Did she look older with her hair down? Maybe. Joan looked at what she was wearing. She thought that wearing jeans instead of a skirt made her look taller. Would she be the shortest girl in her class at Claymore, too?

It would be great not to have to wear a uniform to school. She hoped her parents wouldn't give her a hard time about wearing jeans. Her parents hated jeans. They hated a lot of things that Joan liked — television programs, rock and hip-hop, American movies, and living in the South. Sometimes it seemed to Joan that her mother and father hated everything that she loved.

Joan looked at her watch, grabbed her new red backpack, and headed for the kitchen. Her parents and brother were still at the breakfast table. Her mother was looking over notes for her college lecture and didn't even notice when Joan came into the room. Her thirteen-year-old brother, Adam, glanced up from his cereal and gave Joan the thumbs-up sign. Her father looked up from the book he was reading while he ate breakfast. "Jeans to school?" he said.

"All the girls wear jeans, Father," Adam said. Joan flashed Adam a grateful smile. How lucky that she had a brother who had already been at CMS for a year.

"Mother, we should go," Adam said, "or we'll be late for school."

Michelle Russo looked up from her papers. She seemed surprised to be in the kitchen with her family. Joan wondered if her mother would say something in German or Russian — the two languages she taught at the university.

"Joanie, your hair will fall in your face when you study," her mother finally said — in English. "Shouldn't you put it back?"

"I have a hair clip in my pocket," Joan told her mother.

Ms. Russo put her papers together and dropped them into her briefcase with a sigh. "What a shame there isn't a decent private junior high school around here."

"There are some good teachers at Claymore," Adam said. "Joanie is going to like it there."

"Now that I'm in seventh grade, I want you all to call me *Joan*," Joan told her family. "That's my real name. It's more grown-up."

Paul Chazen smiled at his daughter. "All right, kitten," he said. "Don't forget to sign up for the debate club."

Joan didn't bother to tell her father that she'd outgrown his nickname for her, too.

"The debate club? What is anyone in that school going to have to debate about?" Ms. Russo said. "The merits of basketball versus football? Joanie's and Adam's brains are going to rot in that school."

"Nevertheless," Mr. Chazen told his wife, "the debate club will be good for her."

"Joanie, come on, let's go," her mother said.

"Mother!" Joan exclaimed. "It's *Joan*. That's what you named me, remember?"

"You'll always be *Joanie* to me," her mother insisted. "And as an aside, please do not speak to me in an insolent tone."

Joan knew that there was no way she could win the name battle with her mother.

"Please call me *Joan* at school," Joan told Adam as they walked out of the house together. "That's the way I'm going to introduce myself from now on."

"I'll try," he said and smiled.

Joan looked down at her jeans-clad legs as she climbed into the backseat of the car. All in all, she felt pretty great. She was finally going to CMS. And she was wearing jeans to school.

DOLPHIN COURT APARTMENTS 8:15 A.M.

Melody Max stared at her reflection in the bedroom mirror. She had on a black tank dress. She might be going to school with a bunch of hicks, but she wasn't going to *look* like one. Melody put on her Walkman headphones and hit play. Now, what should she wear on her feet?

Feet. Dancing. Instead of putting on shoes, Melody danced barefoot with her reflection. Suddenly her mother's image appeared in the mirror beside her, scowling and pointing to her watch. Melody pulled off her headphones.

"You are due at your new school in fifteen minutes," Carolyn Sinclair reminded her daughter. "Shouldn't you have some breakfast and get your fancy self moving?"

"It's 8:15!" exclaimed Melody. "Time to see Dad."

Melody grabbed her platform sandals and shoulder bag and rushed out of the room.

Her mother followed. "Do you have to watch him *every* morning on TV?" she asked.

"He's in Miami, and we're over here on the other side of Florida," Melody protested. "It's the only way I can see him now."

"Melody, you know we moved here because I was made editor of the newspaper. That wasn't going to happen in Miami. Please, let's not go over this again." In the sunlit kitchen, Melody saw her mother's beautiful face momentarily crumple into sadness. The divorce had been hard on all of them.

"Sorry," Melody said. "It's just that going to school in Claymore is going to be superboring."

"It's up to you to make it interesting, sugar. Why don't you go out for cheerleading? One of my reporters told me that they have an excellent squad. And it would be a good way to make new friends."

11

"I miss my old friends, Mom."

"I know," her mother said. She poured a glass of orange juice and put it at Melody's place. "I miss my friends, too. But we'll both be fine. Remember, we come from a family of strong women."

"I know," said Melody.

Melody punched on the kitchen television set and poured some cereal into a bowl.

Like magic, there was her handsome dad telling southeastern Florida the weather. She missed Miami, she missed her father, and she missed her friends. She'd e-mail everybody tonight. She'd tell them all about her first day of school in Hicksville. She'd describe how small the school was and the way the kids dressed. Maybe she'd write a memoir: *Hip Girl in Hick Town.*

"Sunny and cool. High in the seventies, low in the sixties," Sydney Max was telling his viewers. "Now let's take a look at the satellite map."

Carolyn Sinclair leaned over and kissed her daughter on the forehead. "I have to go now. Promise me you'll get yourself to school as soon as your father's off the air. And call me when you come home. Have a great day."

Melody didn't believe for a second that she would have a great day.

How could she, when her father and her best

friends were two hundred miles away and she was starting school with a bunch of strangers?

SQUEEZE 8:20 A.M.

Alexis ran the two blocks from her father's apartment to Squeeze, where Emily was waiting for her. "Sorry I'm late," Alexis said breathlessly.

"It's okay, but let's hurry. We can say hi to everybody and find our lockers before homeroom. It's going to be so much fun to change classes!"

Alexis caught her breath, and the two friends ran up the block. "I wish we were in all the same classes," said Alexis. "The building is so big, and there are so many kids I won't know."

"Don't worry," Emily assured her. "You won't get lost. We got that map of the building that came with our welcome to CMS packet. Remember? They are so organized at this school. I love it already."

The two girls turned the corner and saw the pink stucco school building, two stories high. Emily loved how CMS was U-shaped, with a big courtyard of grass and palm trees in the center. It was a much fancier school than her old elementary school.

"I wish we were in the same homeroom at least," said Alexis.

"Me, too," said Emily. "Can you come to my

house and practice cheerleading after school? Lynn said tryouts will probably be this week."

"Okay," agreed Alexis. "My dad won't mind. I'll leave him a message at his office."

Alexis felt better. She'd go home with Emily after school. She and Emily would practice cheerleading in The Manor Hotel ballroom, just like they had all summer. Maybe Emily's parents would invite her to stay for dinner. Even if she wasn't in a lot of classes with Emily, they'd at least have cheerleading together — if they both made it through the tryouts. Alexis looked at the big building and all the kids coming off school buses. There were so many kids at CMS! What if a lot of girls went out for cheering? And what if they were better at it than she was? What if she didn't make the squad and Emily did? Then she'd hardly *ever* see her best friend. Maybe Emily wouldn't even want her for a best friend if they weren't both cheerleaders.

"Look," Emily told Alexis. "There's Jake."

Alexis saw Jake Feder walking toward them. He waved hello, and Alexis waved back. She'd known Jake most of her life, and she liked him a lot. Jake lived with his grandparents in a house behind The Manor Hotel, and he'd been a good friend of Emily's ever since she was three years old and he was five. Sometimes when Alexis felt sorry for herself because her parents were divorced, she remembered Jake's story. His parents and his baby sister died in a fire when Jake was five years old. That's when Jake moved in with his grandparents, who raised him.

Jake draped one arm over Emily's shoulders and the other around Alexis's. Alexis smiled up at him. She loved how his dark hair framed his tan face. " 'Welcome to CMS, place of great learning and great fun,' " he said, quoting the CMS manual. "You're going to love it here."

Alexis suddenly felt happy and excited. Maybe being at CMS wouldn't be so bad after all.

CMS COURTYARD 8:25 A.M.

Sally Johnson stood in the CMS courtyard watching the stream of kids coming off the school buses. Everyone looked so young. Sally guessed that that's what happens when you're in the ninth grade in a seven-through-nine middle school. As she smiled and said hello to old classmates, Sally reminded herself of her goals for the year. She was sure she would be co-captain of the cheerleading squad. Everyone said she was the best cheerleader in the school — even when she was in the eighth grade. It was going to be a great year in cheerleading. She would see to it that CMS placed in the Cheer USA state competitions. She would run for president of the ninth-grade class and probably win. And she wanted to be queen of the CMS prom, too. That would end the school year nicely.

Last year, in eighth grade, Sally dated Dave Grafton, but they broke up over the summer. Now Dave was in high school. If I'm going to reach all of my goals, thought Sally, I have to have a boyfriend right here, at CMS. She spotted Jake Feder. He was the most popular guy in their grade and a terrific basketball player. He also worked part time at Bulldog Café, which was a cool place to hang out. As editor of the school newspaper, Jake could help her with her presidential campaign. Yes, Jake would make an excellent boyfriend.

Sally was surprised to see Jake talking to what were obviously seventh-grade girls. Oh, well, she thought, he couldn't be interested in *them*. Glancing over her shoulder, Sally noticed Darryl Budd coming in her direction. Darryl was captain of the football team and *very* cute. He should be her boyfriend for sure, at least for the football season. Or maybe she'd let him *think* he was her boyfriend while she worked on Jake.

Sally pretended not to see Darryl and headed straight toward Jake. It would be fun to start off the school year with a little jealousy.

Meanwhile, Joan Russo-Chazen was walking through the courtyard with her brother. Adam said hello to some kids as they passed. "Hey, there's Jake Feder," Adam told Joan. "Come on. I'll introduce you."

Joan recognized one of the three girls with Jake. When she first moved to Claymore, she'd taken a Saturday gymnastics class with that red-haired girl. She even remembered that her name was Emily. Joan had loved gymnastics, but her parents decided it was dangerous and a waste of time, so Joan had to drop out of the class. Joan recalled how she and Emily were about the same size two years ago. Now Emily was way bigger. Joan checked out the kids gathering outside the school building. They all looked taller than she was.

A beautiful girl with a blond ponytail was talking to Jake, too. Joan remembered the girl from the school play that Adam was in the year before. She watched her give Jake a hug.

"Who's that?" Joan whispered.

"Sally Johnson," Adam answered.

Joan noticed that her brother was blushing. Her brother must like this girl. And Joan could see why he would.

"Hey, Adam," Jake called. Before she knew it, Joan was being introduced to Jake and Sally.

"This is my sister, Joanie," Adam said. "I mean Joan."

"Which is it," laughed Sally, "Joanie or Joan?"

"My name is Joanie, but they call me Joan,"

said Joan. As soon as she said it she felt like a jerk. Joan was a real name, and Joanie was the nickname. Everybody knew that.

Sally gave Joan a big smile. She has the most beautiful smile, thought Joan. "I think you look like a Joanie," Sally said. "You're so cute. Do you do gymnastics?"

"I just took a few lessons," said Joan. "But I loved it."

"I hope you go out for cheering," Sally told her. "We need a new flyer. You're just the right size. What you don't know, Coach can teach you."

"We're going out for cheering," Emily said to Joan. "I'm Emily. This is Alexis."

A deep male voice from behind Joan interrupted the introductions. Joan turned and faced a very big, very tall, very handsome boy.

"Hi, Darryl," said Sally sweetly. She put her hand casually on his shoulder, got on her tiptoes, and gave him a kiss on the cheek. Joan noticed that her brother blushed again.

Joan listened to the others talking about what they'd done all summer. I'm so shy, she thought. I don't know what to say. Everybody else looks so much older and is so much cooler than I am. A loud buzzer startled Joan, and she jumped. Nobody seemed to notice her surprise. They compared their class schedules as they

18

headed slowly in the direction of the front door. For the moment even her brother had forgotten her.

Joan felt frightened as she followed Adam and his friends into the building.

NORTH DOOR 8:30 A.M.

Alexis noticed that Joan looked a little lost. She's just as nervous as I am, thought Alexis. Alexis slowed down so she and Emily could walk with Joan. "What homeroom are you in?" Alexis asked.

"Room 210," Joan answered.

"Me, too," said Alexis.

"The only time I was in this school was when my brother was in a play," Joan told her. "I'm a little nervous."

Alexis smiled at Joan. "So let's try to sit next to each other in homeroom," she offered.

"I'm in a different homeroom," said Emily. "But maybe our lockers will be near each other."

As they walked down the corridor of seventh-grade lockers, Emily and Alexis said hi to kids they knew from elementary school. "This is Joan," Emily told a couple of girls standing near a locker. Joan smiled and said hi. It was great to hear someone call her by her real name.

The three girls' lockers were in the same row but not next to one another. When Joan saw

Emily and Alexis put their jackets in their lockers, she did the same. Emily took a CMS pendant out of her backpack and stuck it to the inside of her locker door with some Scotch tape. "That's for good luck," she told Joan. "Because I'm trying out for cheerleading."

Then the three girls compared their class schedules. They weren't in many of the same classes, but they all had the same lunch hour.

Another buzzer rang. "That's the signal to go to our homerooms," Emily explained to Joan. She pointed to the end of the corridor. "You and Alexis go that way and up the stairs. I go to a room on this floor right off the main lobby." She added that she'd meet them in the cafeteria at lunch period. "Whoever is first save places for the other two," she suggested. Alexis and Joan agreed and walked down the hall.

Emily followed a group of kids and went toward the lobby. She didn't know any of them. She didn't know as many people at CMS as she thought she would. Emily suddenly felt a little nervous about being in middle school. Don't be silly, she told herself, you were looking forward to this. You wanted to be in middle school.

When Emily reached the lobby, she noticed a girl holding the welcome-to-CMS envelope that all the new students had received in the mail the week before. The girl didn't seem to know which way to go.

Emily went up to her and asked, "May I help you?"

"Sure," Melody Max said. "Where's room 110?"

"On the other side of the lobby," Emily told her. "I'm going to room 109. I'll show you the way." She smiled at the girl. "I'm Emily Granger. I'm new here. I guess you are, too."

"Yeah," said Melody with a sigh. "I am. I just moved here from Miami."

"You'll *love* CMS," Emily gushed as they walked through the lobby. "Everybody has great school spirit. The football team is the best. And girls' basketball won the state championship in their division. So the cheerleaders are real busy going to games."

Emily didn't feel nervous anymore. This was great. She was talking about CMS as if she already went there. Well, now she did. She was on her way to homeroom.

Melody couldn't believe this girl. She was so bubbly and cheerful. Why did everyone in this school smile all the time? Where was their attitude?

"I'm trying out for cheerleading," Emily continued. "Tryouts are this week."

"Good for you," said Melody. She tried to sound enthusiastic, but she was wondering if Emily Whoever-she-was would make the squad. She didn't look very athletic and seemed so young.

"You can go out for cheering if you want," Emily told her. "The squad is great. They do a lot of tumbling and dancing and compete in the Cheer USA competitions. I'm not a cheerleader — yet. But, like I told you, I'm trying out. I just really hope that I get on the squad."

"Well, good luck," said Melody.

"There's your room," Emily said. "See you around."

Emily went into room 109, and Melody went into room 110.

As Melody walked into the room, the teacher was saying, "Okay, everyone, quiet down and listen up." The room went silent. Melody looked around and took the only empty seat.

The boy in the seat behind her smiled. "Hi," he whispered, "I'm Adam." Melody thought Adam had a handsome, sweet face, especially with that smile. Maybe it's not so bad that everyone around here smiles, she thought as she returned the smile and sat down.

"This is room 110, an eighth-grade homeroom," announced the teacher. "Everyone check your schedule to be sure you're in the right room."

Melody Max quickly reached into her pocket and pulled out the paper with her schedule and read, "8:30 A.M. Homeroom. Room 101."

Room 101! She stood up and grabbed her notebook. Everyone looked at her. They were all smiling. Or were they laughing?

Melody held her head high and walked down the aisle out of room 110. She didn't hurry. And she didn't smile. Maybe she could teach these hicks what cool looked like.

CMS CAFETERIA 12 NOON.

Joan was the first of the three girls to reach the cafeteria for lunch period. She wished Emily and Alexis were already there. It would be embarrassing to go into the cafeteria alone. Joan supposed that Emily and Alexis saw a lot of kids from their elementary school in their morning classes. Maybe they wouldn't want to have lunch with her after all. She felt her body tense up. Would she have to eat lunch all by herself?

Joan finally spotted Emily coming down the corridor with a bunch of kids. They were all laughing and talking excitedly to one another, and Emily was the center of the crowd. Emily saw Joan, left the group, and came over to her.

Joan felt her shoulders relax. Emily hadn't forgotten her after all.

"Have you seen Alexis?" Emily asked, looking around.

"Not since second period English," answered Joan.

"Let's go in," Emily suggested. "Alexis will meet us inside."

In the cafeteria line, Emily introduced Joan to some kids. One of them was a girl who had just moved to Claymore. Joan loved the girl's name — Melody Max. She wondered if anyone ever called her Max, but she decided not to ask. Melody Max wasn't very friendly, and when Emily invited her to sit with them, she said, "No, thanks."

Emily found three empty places at the end of a table. "Alexis has a terrible sense of direction," Emily told Joan. "I hope she didn't get lost in the building."

They'd just sat down with their lunches when Joan spotted Alexis coming into the cafeteria. She looked confused until she saw Joan and Emily waving to her. They were already on their chocolate pudding by the time Alexis got her lunch and joined them.

"Did you get lost finding the cafeteria?" Emily asked her.

"Just a little," Alexis admitted. "But wait until you hear what I saw."

"What?" asked Emily and Joan in unison.

"The cheerleaders," answered Alexis excitedly, "putting up posters about the cheerleading tryouts. There's a meeting tomorrow after school for anyone who's interested in cheering. Tomorrow!"

"Tryouts are tomorrow?" asked Emily in astonishment.

"No," Alexis explained, "tryouts start on Friday. Tomorrow is a meeting to talk about the squad and the first cheerleading clinic. Wait till you see the signs. They are so cool. There's one right outside the cafeteria."

"Hurry up," Emily told her. "Eat. Don't talk. Finish your lunch so we can go see it."

While Alexis ate, Emily told Joan she remembered her from the Saturday afternoon gymnastics class they'd taken together. "You were so good," Emily commented. "Why'd you drop out?"

Joan liked Emily, and she wanted to tell her the truth. But the truth was so embarrassing. How could she say that she had to drop out because her parents thought gymnastics was stupid and dangerous? Instead she said, "It was a scheduling problem. I have a piano class then." Which was sort of true, since she now took piano lessons on Saturday afternoons. "I didn't want to drop out though," Joan added with one hundred percent truthfulness. "I really loved gymnastics. I want to take it again someday."

"Sally Johnson said they need another flyer for the cheerleading squad," Alexis mumbled through a mouthful of sandwich. "She should know. She's the best cheerleader on the squad."

"I'm too big to be a flyer," added Emily. "But you're just the right size, Joan. If you like gymnastics, you'll get to do it a lot in cheering. My sister said that the school hires a special coach to work with the squad on gymnastics."

Joan had seen cheerleaders on television and knew what a flyer did. She imagined herself being tossed in the air by a base of cheerleaders. It would be so much fun. It *would* be like flying. But her parents would never let her do that! Joan could imagine their reaction. "Dangerous!" they'd say. "You don't go to school to be thrown in the air. You go to school to learn."

Emily interrupted her thoughts. "Joan, if you're going out for cheerleading, you should come over to my house after school. We're going to practice. My sister Lynn will help us."

"Lynn's a cheerleader in the high school, and she was co-captain of the squad when she was at CMS," added Alexis.

Joan couldn't believe her good luck. She was being asked to someone's house on the first day of school!

In a few minutes the three girls joined the other seventh-graders leaving the lunchroom. A crowd of girls were gathered in front of the cheerleaders' poster in the hall. Even on tiptoes, Joan couldn't read the poster over the heads of the girls in front of her. Suddenly four hands lifted her into the air.

"You feel like a feather," commented Alexis.

"You *have* to go out for cheering," implored Emily.

The three girls read the poster.

WHAT? A meeting and clinic for girls who want to try out for the CMS cheer squad.

WHEN? Tuesday, September 10, at 3:00 P.M.

WHERE? Small gym.

WEAR? Comfortable clothes and athletic shoes.

WHY? Tryouts are Friday, September 13, at 3:45 P.M.

Are you a girl with spirit?
Then let's hear it,
Go, girl, go!

Emily and Alexis put Joan down on the ground.

"Are you going to the meeting?" asked Emily.

Joan nodded. "And I'll practice with you after school," she added excitedly. "If that's still okay."

"It's better than okay," said Emily. "It's great!"

"We can practice stunts with you," added Alexis. "It's perfect."

It is perfect, thought Joan, as she walked to her first afternoon class on her first day at CMS. I'm going to public school. I have two neat new friends. And I'm going to one of their houses after school. Even one of the ninth-grade cheerleaders told me to go out for cheering.

Then Joan had a thought that made her lunch turn over in her stomach. She wanted to be a CMS cheerleader more than anything she had ever wanted in her life. But what if she didn't make the squad? She'd be so disappointed. Then a second thought. If she did make the squad, how could she keep her cheerleading a secret from her parents? Either way she had a huge problem.

CMS COURTYARD 3:05 P.M.

Joan met her brother outside the school as planned. He was talking to that cute ninth-grader, Jake. When Adam saw her, Joan noticed a worried look cross his face. "What's wrong?" she asked.

"I have a drama club meeting," Adam told

her. "You'll have to go home alone. Do you mind?"

Joan laughed. "I was going to say the same thing to you," she told him. "Emily Granger invited me over to her house."

Adam smiled. "Great, Joanie," he said. "I mean *Joan*."

"Maybe I'll see you there later," said Jake. "The Manor Hotel is my second home."

"Great," said Joan. She couldn't get over how friendly everyone was at CMS. Even kids in the ninth grade, like Jake Feder and Sally Johnson.

"What time do you think I have to be home?" she asked Adam.

"Six o'clock," answered Adam. "That was the rule Mother and Father gave me when I started middle school. It should be the same for you."

"Don't worry. I can take care of myself," Joan told him.

"Good," said Adam with relief. "I have enough trouble keeping track of my own schedule. Just call Father and tell him where you are."

Jake laughed. "You're the only kids I know who call their parents *Mother* and *Father*," he said.

"We're the only kids who have parents like our *mother* and *father*," commented Adam.

Joan saw Emily and Alexis coming in their direction. What if they said something about cheering and the tryouts in front of her brother? She wanted to keep cheering a secret from her whole family — for now. "Gotta go," she said as she quickly took off toward her two new friends.

As the girls walked the ten blocks to the Manor Hotel, Emily and Alexis taught Joan a CMS chant Lynn had taught them. Joan loved walking along Main Street with her new friends, chanting and clapping:

Go, blue X X (clap, clap),
Go, White X X (clap, clap),
Fight, Bulldogs, Fight!

Emily and Alexis stopped in front of a huge white-and-yellow building with a big veranda. It looked like a mansion, but it was The Manor Hotel. "Here we are," Emily announced.

Joan had wondered what Emily's house would be like, but she never imagined it would be a hotel!

"We live on the fourth floor," Emily explained. "The second and third floors are where hotel guests stay. The first floor is the lobby, restaurant, café, and the ballroom."

"That's where we practice," Alexis explained. "In the ballroom."

Joan didn't know where to look first when

she walked into the lobby of the Manor Hotel. There were gilt mirrors and huge plants everywhere. Leather couches and chairs were assembled around a fancy-looking red-and-blue rug. The woman at the front desk called out, "How'd it go, sweetie?"

"Great, Mom," Emily called back.

A cute little girl sat on the rug eating cookies. A bulldog crouched beside her. The child was scolding the dog. When she saw Emily she jumped up and ran over to them, yelling, "Bubba ate my cookie. He did." The dog, barking happily, followed her.

Alexis picked up the girl. "Lexis," the little girl whined. "Bubba's going to be sick all over *everything*. He's a bad dog."

Joan was trying not to smile. But it was difficult because the little girl was so cute.

"Lily, you silly," Emily said. "Bubba eats cookies all the time. They don't make him sick."

Lily laid her head on Alexis's shoulder and sighed, "Okay."

"We're going to practice cheering now," Emily told Lily.

"Me, too," Lily announced as she wiggled to get down from Alexis's arms. "And Bubba."

"Only if you're *very* good," Emily told her. "This is a serious practice."

The girls went down the corridor to the ballroom. Lily walked between Alexis and Joan, swinging hands and chanting a CMS cheer.

THE MANOR HOTEL BALLROOM 4:00 P.M.

Joan thought the ballroom was a perfect place to practice. There were large mirrors along one wall. On the other side, afternoon sunlight poured in through floor-to-ceiling windows. Emily went into a closet and took out three purple exercise mats. "You can use my sister's mat," she told Joan. Alexis pulled open the top drawer of a bureau and removed a file folder. "We keep notes on our workouts," she explained.

Joan looked at the calendar of Alexis's and Emily's summer cheerleading practices. How will I ever catch up? she wondered.

"First, we do warm-up exercises," Emily told her.

For the next fifteen minutes the girls did stretches on the mats. Joan loved the workout and promised herself that she would do those exercises every day, whether she was a cheerleader or not. By the end of the warm-up, Bubba and Lily were bored and went off in search of another adventure in the hotel.

In the ballroom the cheerleading practice continued. Alexis and Emily showed Joan basic hand positions. She learned blades, fists, buckets, and candlesticks.

"You're learning everything so *fast*," Alexis told her.

Then they practiced smiling in the mirror. At first Joan felt weird smiling at herself. But when they added a sideline cheer and pretended they were leading Bulldog fans, it wasn't so hard.

By the time Lynn joined them, Joan had learned some arm movements, a few leg positions, and two jumps — the tuck and the spread eagle.

Lynn's great, thought Joan. Emily is so lucky to have an older sister to show her how to do things, like cheering.

The half hour they spent doing tumbling went by in a flash. Joan had been doing somersaults, cartwheels, and front flips on her own ever since she took gymnastics, so those were easy for her. "You are *very* good," Lynn told her. "You'll make a perfect flyer."

"Lynn is a flyer," Alexis told Joan.

"There are other important positions in cheering besides being a flyer," Lynn pointed out.

Emily and Alexis practiced partner stunts with Joan. I love this, Joan thought.

Before Lynn had to leave to do her homework, she told the girls what they should bring to the cheerleading clinic the next day.

If my parents notice my exercise bag, Joan

thought, I'll tell them it's for gym. It is for gym, since the clinic is in the gym. She felt a twinge of guilt. She had never lied to her parents before.

At the end of their practice, the girls walked around the ballroom to cool down. Joan checked her watch. It was 5:30.

Alexis was glad practice was over. She liked the warm-up stretches and some of the jumping. What she didn't really like was yelling. A cheerleader had to project her voice when she cheered. Alexis also felt a little silly when she put on the cheerleaders' smile. It didn't feel natural to her, no matter how much she practiced it. She wished she could enjoy cheerleading as much as she liked playing basketball. But it was great to hang out at the hotel with Emily and have Lynn helping them. Alexis wasn't so sure about Joan yet. It was hard to share her best friend. She hoped Emily wouldn't like Joan better than her. And what if Joan and Emily made the squad and she didn't?

"I have to go home," Joan said.

Good, thought Alexis. Then it will be just me and Emily.

"Where do you live?" Emily asked.

"Delhaven Drive," answered Joan. "It's going to take me quite a while to walk there."

"My street is right next to Delhaven," said

Alexis. "I live on Harbor Road when I'm with my mother. Which is half the time."

"Then we can go home together now," suggested Joan.

"I'm at my dad's this week," explained Alexis. Besides, she thought, I'm not going home now. I want to stay with Emily and her family for as long as I can.

"Why don't you borrow my bike, Joan?" suggested Emily. "You can ride it to school tomorrow."

"That'd be great," said Joan. "I love to bike ride. In fact I'm planning on riding my bike to school a lot."

"So now you can stay here a little longer," said Emily. "Let's go get a soda at the café and decide what we're going wear for the tryout clinic."

As the three girls walked through the lobby toward the cafeteria, Emily put her arm around Alexis's shoulder and asked her if she could stay for dinner.

Alexis had the happy feeling she always did when she knew she'd be having dinner with the Grangers. She smiled at her very best friend in the whole world. "Sure," she said. "I'll call my dad right now."

Alexis went to the front desk to call her father's office.

"Lewis here," her dad answered.

"It's me, Dad," Alexis said.

"Lexi!" he exclaimed. "How'd it go? First day in middle school. Wow!"

"It was okay, Dad," Alexis told him. "I only got lost once."

"How about the teachers? Do you like your teachers?" he asked.

"They're okay, so far. They didn't give us a lot of homework, like I thought they would."

"Good," he said. "Ease into it. That's the way. You home?"

"I'm at Emily's," Alexis told him. "They invited me to dinner, and Emily and I want to do our homework together."

"Great!" said her father. "I mean great for you. I'll work late and get something to eat around here. So don't worry about your old man. I'll pick you up there about nine, okay?"

"Sure," said Alexis. "See you then."

She hung up the phone. Why did her father always sound so happy when she told him she wasn't going to be seeing him? He's probably going to have dinner with one of his girlfriends, she thought. It's a drag for him to have a kid.

Sometimes Alexis wondered if her father was sorry that he had joint custody of her. She knew he loved her, but she wasn't so sure he liked being with her that much. Maybe he'd like it better if she lived with her mother all the time and only saw him on the occasional weekend. But she didn't want to live only with her mother. Her mother was unhappy a lot of the time. For the next few hours she could pretend she lived with the Grangers.

Which is where she *would* live, if she had a choice.

DOLPHIN COURT APARTMENTS 7 P.M.

Melody's mother reached for a third taco. "Thank you, sugar," she said, "for this wonderful meal."

Melody had prepared chicken tacos, avocado and tomato salad, and rice for dinner. Melody knew her mother would be tired and stressed out from her new job. She was glad she could help by having a good meal ready for her. Both Melody's parents had made sure that she learned to cook. "When you have two working parents, you better know how to cook," her father told her the day he taught her how to make taco fillings.

During dinner, Carolyn Sinclair told Melody some stories from the world news that she'd learned during her day at work. Melody was definitely interested. She thought she might be a journalist some day, too. She loved to write.

When her mom asked her about school, Melody didn't say much. She knew her mother didn't want to hear complaints about her new school and classmates. She'd save her complaints for later, when she e-mailed her friends back in Miami.

After dinner Melody went to her room. The apartment was on the second floor of a two-story apartment complex. They had a terrace overlooking a swimming pool. That was nice. And there were tennis courts in the back. But Melody hadn't found anyone to play with. Her favorite tennis partner was her father, and he was in Miami.

Melody looked around her room. Half her boxes were still unpacked, and the walls were bare. The first week she was in Claymore she thought she still might convince her parents to let her move back to Miami. But crying herself to sleep three nights in a row and driving her mother and father crazy with her complaints didn't work. Both of her parents were adamant that she should spend the next three school years in Claymore with her mother and only spend vacations in Miami. Then if she wanted, she could live with her father and go to high school in Miami.

Melody put on some music, turned on her computer, and went on-line. First she checked for messages. There was one from her dad.

Maxi's Maxim for the day: Put your best foot forward and you won't fall down.

Melody smiled to herself. Her father was always making up phrases like that. It was his way of giving advice. But that was all he said in his e-mail. Short but sweet, sort of.

There were no other messages. Had her friends forgotten her so fast? Melody reread some old e-mail messages and checked the dates. Two weeks ago, when she first moved to Claymore, her friends e-mailed her almost every day, like they promised. But she hadn't heard from any of them for two days. Well, she'd write to them. She hadn't forgotten *them*.

Hey, out there. Cheers from the lost girl on the Gulf Coast. I'm marooned here with a bunch of hicks. No soul. No hip-hop. No fun. Where did all the dancing go? Here's the scoop about my first day at Claymore Bore-more Middle School. Young. Everyone looks so young. Except a few guys and gals in the ninth grade. Wish I could go home to you all

and the fun we used to have. How's the hip-
hop class, and what concerts are you all
catching? Write and let me know there's a
big old world over there in Miami that will still
be there when I finish my three-year prison
term. I'll be back for a long weekend at
Thanksgiving. Cannot wait to see you all.
Love ya. The Max.

Melody sent the letter to five of her best
friends in Miami but decided against sending
it to her dad. He was sick of her complaints
as much as her mother was. Instead, she sent
him:

Trying to put that best foot forward. Get rid of
the tie you wore on the air this morning. It is
way old-fashioned, but not old enough to be
cool. Love ya. The Max.

Next Melody tackled her homework. She ac-
tually enjoyed the English assignment, reading
a short story and answering some questions.
She was finished by nine o'clock. What would
she do next? She wasn't in the mood for television. She looked around her room. Maybe she'd
hang some of her favorite concert posters and
put her books on the bookshelves. She opened

the blinds. She liked the way the lighted pool bounced aqua light into her room.

Melody revved up the volume on her stereo and went to work unpacking boxes and decorating her room.

CMS SMALL GYM. TUESDAY 3:05 P.M.

After their last class, Emily, Alexis, and Joan went to the locker room and changed into their cheerleading practice clothes. They walked into the gym together and sat on the front row of bleachers.

At 3:30 Emily turned around and made a quick count of the girls. There were about twenty on each of the three rows of bleachers. That meant sixty girls were thinking about trying out for ten positions on the squad! What if they all tried out? With that much competition, what were her chances of making the squad? Or Alexis's? Or Joan's? What were the chances of all three of them making the squad? All the practicing she and Alexis had done during vacation had to pay off. Didn't it?

"There are a lot of people here," Alexis whispered in Emily's ear.

"I know," Emily whispered back.

The door at the side of the gym flung open, and Coach Carmen Cortes came running into the room. She was followed by the six ninth-grade cheerleaders. Emily thought they all looked great in their blue-and-white cheerleading uniforms.

Coach Cortes stopped dead center in front of the stands of girls. The cheerleaders organized themselves in a row behind her.

Coach Cortes looked over the crowd of girls. Her gaze stopped when she saw Emily. "So we have another Granger in the school," she said. "How's Bubba IV?"

"Great!" answered Emily.

"Let's hear it for Bubba," Coach shouted to the cheerleaders.

"Bubba, Bubba," Sally Johnson called out through the megaphone.

The rest of the cheerleaders joined in with:

Bubba, Bubba,
Lead the fight.
Bubba, Bubba,
Help us win.
Fight! Win! Fight!

The girls who knew that Bubba was the CMS mascot cheered. Coach Cortes explained who Bubba was to the rest.

This is great, thought Emily. The school mascot lives in my house. But the great feeling didn't last. She had a terrible thought. What if the other girls thought she thought she'd make the squad because the school mascot was her dog? She knew that wasn't true. The judges for the tryouts came from other towns and wouldn't even know the names of the girls trying out. But did everyone else understand that? Maybe they'd think that Coach Cortes could influence the vote. Could she?

"All right, girls," Coach said. "Here's the drill. First, I'll explain what is required of a CMS cheerleader. By the way, the eighth-graders on the squad have to try out again. That's why they're sitting in the bleachers with you. So, seventh-graders, those of you who make the squad will have to try out again next year." A few people moaned. "The current ninth-graders will demonstrate some of the moves we use in our cheers so you can see what we expect of you. After that we'll conduct the first of three clinics. The clinic sessions run for an hour after school today, tomorrow, and Thursday. Tryouts are on Friday. Results will be posted outside this gym as soon as the votes are tallied."

Coach Cortes took a few steps forward and silently looked over the girls on the bleachers. Did she smile extra special at me? wondered Emily.

"After today," Coach continued, "you may decide against trying out. That's okay. Cheering isn't a sport for everyone. Don't try out unless you want to be a cheerleader with all your heart. Understood?"

Emily looked around. Many girls were nodding their heads.

"So are you ready?" shouted the coach in a strong cheerleader's voice.

"Yes!" shouted the gathering of girls.

"Give us a C," one of the ninth-graders chanted.

"C!" answered the tryout girls.

"Give us an M," chanted all the cheerleaders.

"M!" the crowd shouted back to them.

"S!" called the cheerleaders.

"S!"

"What do you have?"

"CMS!"

"Louder," called the cheerleaders.

"CMS!" chanted the crowd.

OUTSIDE THE GYM DOORS 3:15 P.M.

Melody stood by the gym doors watching. Emily waved for her to come in and sit next to her. She pushed closer to the girl next to her to show Melody that there was enough room.

If I sit down, thought Melody, everyone will think I'm trying out for cheerleading — which

44

I'm not. She shook her head no. She'd stay right where she was. She wanted to see what else happened at a cheerleading tryout meeting in Boremore. It'd make great material for tonight's e-mail to her friends in Miami.

Melody watched the cheerleaders demonstrate jumps, some tumbles, and lifts. Next they performed some very cool dance moves to an intricate beat of pretty good music. Melody had to admit that the ninth-grade cheerleaders were impressive. The only thing she didn't like was their constant smiling. They could use a little attitude.

As Melody watched the dance, she moved her own body to the beat of the music. When the demonstration was finished, everyone — including Melody — clapped. At the same time she checked out the expressions on the faces of the girls in the bleachers. She'd bet anything a lot of those girls were thinking, I could never do what those cheerleaders did. No way.

But I can, Melody thought. I can do somersaults and cartwheels. And I bet I could learn how to do a flip. I wouldn't be a flyer, but I'd be good at being the base for one. I have strong arms and legs, and I'm very steady. And with practice, I could do that dance routine. Melody wondered if the team had a dance choreographer working with them, because whoever was making up the steps was good.

Two things simultaneously interrupted Melody's thoughts. One was the sudden presence of someone by her side. The other was the voice of the coach saying, "You must all be wondering how our cheerleaders got to be so good."

I am, thought Melody. She ignored the person beside her and listened to the coach.

"How do we do it, squad?" the coach asked her cheerleaders.

"Practice. Practice. Practice," they chanted.

"And more practice," added Coach Cortes. "We also have some outside help. High school cheerleaders assist in our practices. And there is a dance coach and a gymnastics consultant who gives special classes in tumbling."

So there *is* a special dance teacher, thought Melody.

She turned slightly and came face-to-face with a big, handsome guy with the bluest eyes she had ever seen.

"Hey," the boy said in a low voice. "You going out for cheering?"

Melody shook her head no.

"I saw you dancing there a minute ago," he said. "Way cool. You should go out for cheering."

"Who are you?" Melody whispered. "And why are you telling me what I should do?"

Darryl, surprised that she spoke to him so boldly, took a step back.

"Darryl," he whispered back. "I think you're good so you should try out. They lost a lot of great cheerleaders."

"Lost?" Melody asked.

"Not lost-lost," he said. "They graduated. They went to high school." He smiled at her. "Who are you?"

"Melody," she answered. "I'm new here."

"I know," he said.

"How do you know?" she asked.

"I would have noticed you before."

"Darryl," the coach called. "Darryl Budd, the captain of our football team, has a few words to say."

Melody knew that in this school being the captain of the football team was probably a very big deal. "Captain, huh," she commented. "Way cool." She finally gave Darryl a smile — a little one.

When she looked away from him, she saw that everyone in the gym was looking at Darryl . . . and at her.

"Darryl, get over here and tell these tryout girls what it means to the football team to have a cheer squad."

The cheerleaders chanted, **"Dar-ryl. Dar-ryl. Dar-ryl."**

Darryl jogged across the floor to the center of the gym. He stood with spread legs, hands on hips, a big smile on his face. There is no denying that he's cute, thought Melody. And he knows it.

"Try out for the squad," Darryl told the prospective cheerleaders. "We need a strong cheer squad out there helping us win. Then, when the cheer squad goes to Cheer USA competitions, the football and basketball players will be out there cheering for you."

The cheerleaders and the coach broke up laughing. "I better explain," said the coach. "Last year the football team showed up at the state cheerleading competitions in girls' cheerleading uniforms. They even performed a cheer. It was a unique experience. To say the least."

Melody, imagining Darryl in a skirt doing cheerleading motions and jumps, laughed, too. She was glad to see that people at Boremore Middle School had a sense of humor.

"What we did was a joke," Darryl said. "But cheerleading is a serious sport. And the other athletes respect you. So go for it."

Melody was impressed by Darryl. She thought it would take a lot of confidence and a good sense of humor for a football player to put on girls' clothes.

The crowd applauded him as he ran off the floor.

Melody thought Darryl would leave the gym. But he stood next to her while Coach Cortes told the girls to organize themselves in groups of ten around the gym.

"Anyone who knows that they don't want to try out should leave now," Coach announced.

Some girls left the gym. According to Melody's calculations, that left about fifty or so girls to try out for ten positions on the squad.

As the tryout girls were moving into groups, Sally came over to Darryl and draped an arm around his shoulder. "You waiting for me, baby?" she asked Darryl.

She ignored Melody.

"You want me to?" asked Darryl.

Melody was surprised that Sally was ignoring her and that Darryl didn't introduce her. Darryl and Sally seemed to only have eyes for each other.

When Sally did glance in her direction, Melody said, "I'm Melody Max. New here. Seventh grade." Did Sally relax when Melody told her she was in the seventh grade? Melody wondered. Or was that her imagination?

"Sally Johnson," said Sally. "*Ninth* grade."

"Tell Melody she should go out for cheering,"

Darryl told Sally. "I know she'd be good." He gave Melody a huge smile.

Sally smiled at Melody, too. "Are you going to try out?" she asked.

Melody said, "I don't think so."

Sally looked Melody over. She was much too pretty. And Darryl clearly liked her. You may only be in the seventh grade, thought Sally, but I don't trust you. And I sure don't trust Darryl. He loves to have pretty girls falling all over him. Well, I'm the prettiest girl on the squad, and I intend to keep it that way. Sally continued to smile at Melody as she had these thoughts.

Melody was thinking about how friendly Sally was when she noticed Emily and two other girls running toward them.

"Hi," Emily said cheerfully. "Melody, these are my friends. You already met Joan. This is Alexis. We're all going out for cheering."

Melody said hi.

"So aren't the CMS cheerleaders great?" Emily asked.

"They are," Melody admitted.

"Are you going to try out?" Joan asked her.

Before Melody could answer Darryl said, "Sure she is. Aren't you, Melody?" He winked at her.

"She shouldn't do it if she doesn't want to," said Sally.

"At least take the clinic," suggested Emily. "Then you'll know if you like it or not. You'll never know if you don't try."

Coach Cortes walked over to them. "You four," she told Emily, Alexis, Joan, and Melody. "Go over with that group of six." She pointed across the gym to a huddle of girls. "Put a move on. We have a lot of work to do."

The coach thinks I'm doing the clinic, thought Melody. I might as well. I don't have anything else to do this afternoon. Taking the clinic doesn't mean I'll have to try out. What do I have to lose?

CMS SMALL GYM 3:30 P.M.

In a few minutes Coach explained to the cheerleader hopefuls how the clinic would be run. First, there would be a fifteen-minute warm-up for everyone. Then the tryout girls would break up into their groups of ten. The ninth-grade cheerleaders would coach the groups in different parts of the gym. Each group would go from station to station.

Mae Lee, a tall, thin girl with long, straight black hair, would run the jump station. Elvia Gignoux, a short, dark-haired cheerleader, would teach a dance routine. Cynthia Jane Morris, CJ, a small girl, was responsible for teaching tumbling. And Sally would teach the center cheer. Two high school cheerleaders came into the gym. They were there to help CJ with the tumbling.

"All right, everyone," shouted Carmen Cortes to the fifty girls lined up in front of her. "Let's go! Feet hip-width apart. Arms up. Stretch to the right! And breathe out. One. Two. Three. Four."

After the fifteen-minute warm-up, the groups went to the stations. The group that Emily, Alexis, Joan, and Melody were in went to Sally Johnson first to learn a required cheer.

When they went to the jump station, Emily saw that Joan was already jumping higher and better than she and Alexis. And Melody! She practically flew in the air. No one had to tell her to point her toes or the right placement of her head. It was hard to believe she'd never cheered before.

"I studied a lot of ballet," she told Emily as they left Mae's station and headed toward the tumbling station. "And there's a lot of jumping in that." Melody was sweating from the workout and smiling. Emily was glad Melody was finally having some fun at CMS.

Sally watched Melody walking across the gym floor with her friends. She's too pretty and she's too good, she thought. Sally also saw that Darryl was still on the sidelines. She waved to him, but he didn't see her. He was looking elsewhere. Sally followed his gaze and saw that he was watching Melody, too. Darryl was obviously interested in Melody. I can't let that girl make the squad, thought Sally.

I don't know how I'll do it, but I'm keeping Melody Max off my squad.

DOLPHIN COURT APARTMENTS 5:30 P.M.

When Melody got home she was surprised at how terrific her bedroom looked. She'd forgotten that she'd fixed it up the night before. She took off her clothes and put on her bathing suit. Her body felt loose and strong. She'd go for a swim in the pool to cool off. I haven't felt this good since I moved to Claymore, she thought. Cheering is fun. And tonight she and her mom could have a cookout by the pool. It was pretty neat how Dolphin Court Apartments had a gas grill near the pool that all the tenants could use. Maybe one of her new cheerleading friends played tennis. She liked Sally. I'll probably hang out with her and her friends instead of other seventh-graders, Melody thought as she ran down the outside stairs to the pool. And then there was that cute guy, Darryl.

Living in Claymore might not be so bad after all.

THE MANOR HOTEL 6:00 P.M.

Tuesday nights, Emily's mother was maître d' in the restaurant, and her father manned the front desk, so the Granger kids ate in the hotel dining room. Emily's entire body ached, and she'd never felt so hungry in her life. She was tired and cranky from the long day at school, topped by the two-hour cheerleading clinic. Her sister asked her how she did in the tryout clinic.

"It was fun," Emily told her through a mouthful of fried chicken. "Really fun."

Emily didn't tell Lynn that she felt discouraged about her chances for making the CMS cheerleading squad. That it seemed like everyone was so much better than she was. Or that she envied her sister who was already so grownup and such a great cheerleader. What if I don't make the squad? wondered Emily. What if I'm the first Granger who isn't a Bulldog athlete?

"Is there anything you need extra help with?" Lynn asked. "I can help you after dinner."

"I have a lot of homework," Emily told her. "Maybe tomorrow night."

Emily took the last bite of her mashed potatoes. Eating the smooth, buttery potatoes made her feel better. As she reached for a second helping of potatoes, she eyed the chocolate cake on the dessert table. She could eat more and still have room for dessert.

SEAVIEW TERRACE 6:30 P.M.

Alexis looked in the freezer at her father's house. There were four different frozen dinners for her to choose from. Her father wasn't going to be home until nine. "Microwave yourself something, honey," he said on the message he'd left for her on the answering machine.

Alexis picked out lasagna. As she went to open the microwave she saw her reflection in the glass door. She looked upset. Alexis the worrywart, her father sometimes called her. Well, he should have seen her today at the cheerleading clinic. Her jaw hurt from smiling so much. She placed the frozen meal in the microwave and set the timer for five minutes.

While her meal was being zapped, Alexis stood at the window and stared out at the Gulf of Mexico. Waves tumbled gently against the shore and rolled back out.

"Big blue! Is here! Stand up and cheer!" Alexis chanted loudly.

Yell GO. FIGHT. WIN.
GO, FIGHT, WIN!
Hey Blue! Let's fight!

Yell fight. Bulldogs. Fight!
Go, big Blue and White. Let's win
tonight!

By the end of the chant, Alexis's voice had dropped to a whisper and tears filled her eyes. It was no use. She didn't have the spirit. Everyone would know it, and she wouldn't make the squad.

The bell on the microwave rang. Time for dinner. Alone.

DELHAVEN DRIVE 6:45 P.M.

Tuesday was French night in the Russo-Chazen household. Everyone spoke French at dinner. Joan hoped that her parents wouldn't ask her what she did after school. Then she wouldn't have to lie to them.

If I do have to lie, she thought, maybe it will be easier in a foreign language.

Joan kept the French conversation away from her. She asked her father to describe the book that he was translating. She asked her mother about her students. And she asked Adam about his English class and what books they would be reading this semester. She did it all in French, but she didn't pay too much attention to their answers. She was going over chants for cheers in her head as she ate. After each answer she practiced her smile on her family.

"Joanie, why are you grinning like that?" her mother asked in French.

"I smile because I am happy," Joan answered in French. Which was one hundred percent the truth in any language.

When they'd finished dinner, her parents — who had prepared that night's meal — went to the living room to read and listen to classical music. All Joan had to do was clean up the kitchen with Adam. Then she could go to her room to do her homework. She'd be home free, lie free.

Joan knew that sooner or later she'd have to tell Adam that she was trying out for the CMS cheerleading squad. He went to CMS, so he'd find out. Besides, she would need his help to convince her parents to let her be a cheerleader. But tonight she wanted to keep it a secret to herself. Her big, wonderful secret — that Sally Johnson said that of all the girls who were going out for cheering, Joan was the best candidate to be the new CMS squad flyer!

CMS SMALL GYM. WEDNESDAY 5:00 P.M.

At the end of their second day of the clinic, the cheerleading hopefuls lined up in two rows in the center of the gym. Nine girls had dropped out after the first clinic, so now there were thirty-six. The workshop leaders sat on the bleachers with Coach Cortes and watched the girls do the required cheer.

After the last **"Fight, Bulldogs, fight,"** Coach leaned toward Sally and whispered. "Did you see that girl in the center of the back row?"

Sally knew that Coach was talking about Melody Max and nodded.

"I like her style," Coach said. "She has great energy and attitude. Her jumps are high and light with soft, bouncy landings."

Sally thought she had coached Melody so that Coach Cortes *wouldn't* like her. She'd told Melody to show as much attitude as she wanted. She thought that Coach Cortes wouldn't like Melody's jazzy style and that Melody would stick out as not being a good team player. But the plan had backfired! Melody looked good out there. She had a fabulous jump. Keeping Melody off the squad was going to be more difficult than Sally thought. Plan A had not worked. It was time to move on to plan B.

When the tryout girls went to the locker room to change, Sally followed them. She caught up with Melody and Alexis.

"Hey, good work, you guys," she told them. "How do you like cheering so far?"

"Great," said Melody with a big smile.

"Yeah," said Alexis. "And it's fun to be with all your friends after school."

"Well, show that spirit, okay, Alexis?" said Sally. "Give it your all."

"That's what I want," said Alexis. "To give it my all."

"Melody," said Sally. "I think we live in the same direction. You're at Dolphin Court Apartments, right?"

"That's right," said Melody.

"If you're going home now, we could walk together," Sally told her.

"Sure," said Melody. She tried to sound cool, but inside she was thrilled. Sally Johnson, a ninth-grade cheerleader, wanted to walk home with her.

"Meet you in front of the school," Sally said with a big smile.

As Melody quickly changed her clothes, she thought about her first three days at CMS. She liked Emily and her friends much more than she thought she would. Emily and Joan might look young, but they were very sweet and seemed genuinely nice. And Alexis Lewis, who looked more mature, also had divorced parents. She and Melody had already had a talk about that. So I know three seventh-graders who could be my friends, Melody thought.

But to have friends in the ninth grade would be so cool. Darryl Budd seemed interested in her. He had walked her home after the first clinic. She had an interesting talk with Emily's friend Jake Feder about music before school that morning. Now Sally Johnson was walking home with her!

If she made the cheerleading squad, life in Claymore might not be half bad.

CMS COURTYARD 5:10 P.M.

Melody walked out of school a few minutes later. Joan, Emily, and Alexis were standing around talking with two guys. Emily motioned for her to come over. Melody recognized the cute dark-haired guy. He was the eighth-grader who had smiled at her when she was in the wrong homeroom.

"Hi, again," Adam said when Emily introduced them. He smiled broadly. While the other girls were telling Jake Feder about the cheer clinic, Adam whispered to Melody, "You were amazingly cool about homeroom Monday morning."

You're pretty cool yourself, thought Melody.

When Sally came out of the building a few minutes later she saw Jake and Adam talking with Emily, Alexis, Joan, and Melody. They were all laughing and gabbing like best friends. Sally watched them for a few seconds before they saw her. Jake and Adam were paying special attention to Melody, Sally was sure of it. That girl could easily become the most popular girl at school — and she was only a seventh-grader!

As Sally ran up to the group she covered her real feelings with a cheerful laugh, and said, "Hey, everybody."

Minutes later, Melody and Sally were walking along Shore Road. Sally knew that Melody felt like a big deal walking home with a cheerleader. It was time to put part one of plan B into action.

"That was the first time Coach Cortes saw you do the required cheer," Sally told Melody. "She said something about you to me."

"What'd she say?" Melody asked. "I hope it was good."

"I don't want to upset you or anything," Sally said in a concerned tone, "but Coach said that you were showing off. I thought I should tell you she really hates show-offs."

"But you said to show my stuff," Melody protested.

"I said to show your stuff," said Sally. "I didn't say to show off. There's a big difference."

"There is?"

"Oh, yeah," Sally told her. "I thought you understood that, Melody. A cheerleader is supposed to blend in. Keep an eye on how sharp the other girls are doing their motions. How high they're jumping. You stood out too much, Mel. Show you have team spirit."

Melody looked very concerned. "Thanks for telling me," she said.

"Well, I want to help you," Sally told her.

"Did Coach say anything else?" Melody asked warily.

"No," replied Sally. "But I noticed something."

"What?"

"Your jumps," Sally said sadly. "You're jumping higher than the girls next to you. That's the show-off thing. And you're springing too much when you come down. Land with authority. *Stick it* means to *land it*."

"But Mae Lee said to keep the landings light," said Melody, "so you'll be ready for the next move."

"It's difficult to keep it light and land with authority. But that's why everyone who tries out for cheering doesn't make the squad," Sally explained.

"I see," said Melody. But Sally could tell she was confused. Confusion. Lack of confidence. Perfect.

"Do me a favor, Melody," Sally told her. "Don't tell anyone I told you what Coach said or that I gave you advice. I just saw an opportunity to improve your chances for making the squad."

"Thanks for telling me," said Melody.

Sally gave Melody her warmest, most sincere-seeming smile. "I like you," she said. "I'm here to help you, Mel."

NINTH-GRADE LOCKER AREA.
THURSDAY 8:15 A.M.

Sally was talking with her friends, but she kept an eye out for Jake Feder. It was time to put part two of plan B into action. When she finally spotted him, she headed in his direction.

"Hey, Jake," she said when they met. "I'll wait for you. We can go to homeroom together."

Jake's eyes sparkled, and a smile spread across his face. "Okay," he said.

He's thrilled to walk to homeroom with me, Sally thought. I haven't lost my power.

She stood close to Jake as he opened his locker. When he took a Walkman and a tape out of his pocket, Sally noticed the title of the tape. "The Raves," she said. "You like them?"

"Don't know," said Jake. "Melody just lent it to me. They're the hot thing in Miami right now. She went to a concert and got hooked."

"I'll have to check them out," said Sally.

Jake took out a couple of books, put the Walkman and tape in his locker, and slammed the door shut. "Melody's trying out for cheering," he said enthusiastically. "I heard she's good."

"Not," said Sally.

"Not?" he said, surprised.

Sally put on a concerned look. "People should stop telling her she's good. I'm afraid she's in for a big disappointment."

"But Emily and Alexis said . . ." began Jake.

"What do they know, Jake?" Sally said as they started down the hall side by side. "They're seventh-graders. They're just learning about cheering themselves. Melody just isn't good enough, Jake. And even if she was good, I don't think she should be on the squad."

"Why not?" Jake asked with concern.

"I can't say," Sally told him.

Jake stopped on the stairs. "What did she do?" he asked.

"It's not what she did, Jake," said Melody thoughtfully. "It's her attitude. It's what she says."

"Sally, come on, tell me," Jake said.

"Melody Max is a phony," Sally told him. "I hate to say it, but she makes fun of everyone behind their back."

"She does?" Jake said incredulously.

They continued up the stairs. "She does," said Sally sadly. "I was surprised, too. The only reason she's interested in cheering is because it's a way to stay in shape. Basically she thinks we're all a bunch of hicks. She's just killing time until she can move back to Miami."

"But she's so friendly," Jake protested. "Especially to Emily and Alexis."

They'd reached their homeroom, and Sally put a hand on Jake's arm to stop him in the doorway. There was more she wanted to tell him. Besides, Darryl was already in the room, and she wanted him to see her and Jake having an intimate conversation. She took a step closer to Jake. "The thing is, Jake," she whispered, "Melody knows that the Grangers are connected to the CMS sport scene. She also knows that Emily's sister helps them with cheerleading practices. I think she's using Emily to try to get on the squad. But behind Emily's back she makes fun of her. Melody calls her 'that chubette' and thinks Emily's silly with all her school spirit."

"Wow," said Jake.

"At first I was fooled by Melody, too," Sally told Jake. "But trust me, she's not what she seems." She looked at her feet. "I feel just awful for Emily," she muttered.

"And Emily's been so nice to her," Jake commented.

"I don't like to talk about people behind their backs," Sally told him. "Maybe I'm wrong about

Melody. She just moved here and everything. I wouldn't want anyone to be mean to her because of something I said."

"Don't worry, Sally," Jake said. "I won't repeat it. I'm just glad I know."

The second bell rang.

Jake stood back to let Sally go into the room first. He's such a gentleman, Sally thought. It must kill him to think that someone is backstabbing his little friend Emily Granger.

She was right. As Jake went to his seat and listened to homeroom announcements, all he thought about was Emily. She was exactly the age his baby sister would be if she hadn't died in the fire. When he'd moved in with his grandparents, he thought of her as a sister. Now someone was making a fool of Emily and using her to get what they wanted. He had to protect Emily from Melody. But how?

NORTH CORRIDOR 3:05 P.M.

Melody walked slowly through the lobby toward the small gym. The day before, she had been excited and confident about cheering. Now she was disappointed and scared. The tryouts were the next day, and she was doing everything wrong. Last night she tried doing jumps the way Sally described, but they felt awkward and heavy. My first mistake was comparing cheer jumps to ballet leaps, thought Melody. Or maybe my first mistake was going out for cheering. Maybe I'm not cut out to be a cheerleader.

Jake came out of a classroom and cut in front of Melody. She was sure he saw her, but he kept walking. "Hey, Jake," she called out. "Wait up."

He turned and waited for her, but he didn't smile or say hi. Was it her imagination, or was he trying to avoid her?

"Have you seen Emily?" he asked.

"I'm meeting her in the locker room," Melody told him. "We have tryout clinic."

"Oh," he said. He seemed disappointed.

"Is everything okay?" she asked.

"Yeah, sure," he said. He turned and ran ahead of her toward the small gym.

Why doesn't he want to walk there with me? Melody wondered. She quickened her own step. She had to shake herself out of this bad mood. Two days ago she didn't care about the kids at Claymore or about cheerleading. Now her heart was set on being on the cheer squad, and her feelings were hurt because someone didn't say hi to her.

Emily, Alexis, and Joan were already in the locker room when she got there.

Alexis looked up from tying her athletic

shoes. "I'm so nervous," she told Melody. "This is our last chance to learn this stuff before tryouts."

"We're nervous, but we're still having fun," added Joan.

Melody looked around at her new friends. Alexis. Joan. Emily. She would like to become better friends with all of them. But after tryouts tomorrow I probably won't be part of this group, she thought. Everyone will be a CMS cheerleader but me.

Alexis had the same thought.

So did Emily.

Joan was pretty confident she could make the squad. But she didn't know if her parents would let her be a cheerleader.

The four girls went into the gym together and lined up with the other cheerleader hopefuls for the warm-up.

As Emily took her place between Alexis and Melody, she noticed Jake standing near the bleachers. He was motioning for her to come over. Emily was halfway to Jake when Coach Cortes came into the gym blowing her whistle to signal the start of the warm-up. Emily waved to Jake and went back to her place. She wondered what he wanted. She'd call him as soon as she got home.

It was during the jump workshop with Mae Lee that Emily first noticed the change in

Melody's cheering. Her jumps weren't as high as they were the day before. She was also landing with a thud. Maybe it's just jumps that are giving her trouble, thought Emily.

Next they had the center cheer workshop with Sally. Sally told them to take turns performing the cheer in groups of threes. When Melody's group was performing it, Emily noticed that she kept looking at the girls on either side of her instead of at the imaginary crowd. It's like Melody's a whole different cheerleader from the one she was yesterday, thought Emily. There is no way she's going to make the squad if she cheers this way for the tryouts.

Emily also noticed that Melody was quiet when they were leaving the building and saying good-bye to one another outside of school. Emily was nervous about the tryouts, too. And so was Alexis. Even Joan, who was doing so well with the tumbling and had a terrific shot at being picked, seemed to be worried.

As she walked home alone Emily thought over her chances for making the squad and decided they weren't very good. All she could think was, What if I don't make it? From the time she was Lily's age she had wanted to be a CMS cheerleader, just like her mother and older sister. Now it was her turn, and she wasn't going to make it.

Her dream would be gone like a puff of smoke.

BULLDOG CAFÉ 5:45 P.M.

Emily was so distracted by her own mood that she didn't even notice Jake when she walked by Bulldog Café on her way into the hotel.

"Hey, Em," Jake called out. "I've been waiting for you."

Emily turned and saw Jake sitting at the outside corner table. She said hi as she went over and sat in the chair across from him.

"What's wrong?" he asked. "You look sort of sad."

Emily quickly replaced her worried look with a big Emily smile. "Nothing. Nothing's wrong."

Jake leaned forward and looked deep into her eyes. "Emily, it's me," he said. "You don't have to pretend."

"I guess I'm tired and hungry," she said.

"What do you want?" he asked. "I'm having a yogurt smoothie with mango and banana."

"That sounds perfect," she said. "And a donut."

Jake pushed his smoothie toward her and stood up. "Have this one," he said. "I'll get another. Chocolate donut?"

She nodded. "Thanks, Jake," she said. "You're great."

"Sure," he said.

By the time Jake returned with the second smoothie and the donut, Emily was ready to talk about what was on her mind.

"This was our last clinic before tryouts," she began. "I guess I'm real nervous. But all my friends are nervous, too. Especially Melody. Something weird is going on with her."

"I was afraid Melody would upset you," Jake said.

"You were?" she asked. "Why?"

"I have this feeling that Melody might be a little . . . phony," Jake said. "I know you've been really friendly with her. That's why I came to the gym today — to tell you that I thought that."

"Phony?" said Emily with surprise. "Melody? I don't think she's phony. Just the opposite. I think she's honest. And I thought she was going to be a terrific cheerleader. But today she seemed to have lost her confidence, and she was making mistakes all over the place. It's like she's a different person."

"Maybe she *is* a different person from the one you think she is," said Jake. "I mean, we hardly know her. And she did just move here from Miami. I don't think she's so thrilled to be living in Claymore."

"Oh, that," said Emily. "That's the way she felt when she first got here. She told me all about it. But now that she's making friends and trying out for cheering, she's happy. Or she was until today."

"I don't think you should worry so much about Melody," said Jake. "The important thing is that you go out there tomorrow and do *your* best at the tryouts."

"But I'm afraid I'm not good enough, Jake," Emily confessed. "There are so many girls who are terrific. You should see Adam's sister, Joan. She is so great."

"Em," said Jake imploringly. "You practiced all summer. Now all you can do is give it your all. If you don't make it, you don't make it. It won't be the end of the world."

In a flash Emily saw the out-of-town games she wouldn't go to. The Cheer USA competitions she wouldn't be in. The pep rallies. The parades. It would be the end of the Granger family tradition of Bulldog athletes and the life she planned for herself. Tears welled in her eyes.

Jake leaned forward. "Em, we have to get you out of this negative thinking mode," he said. "It's time for some positive thinking. Remember how you helped me when I was so nervous about being in the play last year?"

"How'd I help you?" Emily asked.

"You practiced that play with me for hours," he answered. "You took all those parts."

"Are you going to practice cheerleading with me?" Emily asked with a little giggle.

"No," said Jake. "But I think you should do what my grandmother is always telling me to do. You should write something."

"Write something?" Emily said.

"Write down your thoughts," Jake told her.

"Okay," Emily agreed. She opened her backpack and took out a notebook and pencil. "What do I write?"

"You should probably make some kind of list," he said.

"I know," Emily said. " 'Ten Ways to Cope If I Don't Make the Squad.' "

"You're kidding, right?" said Jake.

"Yes," she admitted. "Sort of." She thought for a second. "I'll make a list of things you should remember when you're going for tryouts. I'll call it 'Tryout Tips.' "

"That's more like it," Jake said.

As Emily made the list she explained why each of her ideas was an important tryout tip.

When she had completed the list, Jake read the whole thing out loud.

CHEERLEADING TRYOUT TIPS

1. Concentrate on your own performance. Don't worry about what the other girls are doing.
2. Have a positive, confident attitude and project it.
3. Look at the judges and smile.
4. Exaggerate your moves. Make it SHARP!
5. Project your voice and emphasize key words in the cheer.
6. Make jumps high, point toes, land light, SMILE.
7. If you make a mistake, go on as if nothing went wrong.
8. Do your personal best, and know that your best is the best you can do.

"I feel better," said Emily. "Thanks, Jake." She took the last sip of her smoothie. "I'm going to call Alexis, Joan, and Melody right away and tell them about my tryout tips. Maybe it will help them keep the tryout jitters under control, too. Especially Melody."

"Don't worry about Melody, Emily," said Jake.

"Jake, that doesn't sound like you!" Emily exclaimed.

"I doubt that she's worrying about you," Jake said. "Call Alexis and Joan. But let Melody Max take care of herself. I am sure she can."

"You really don't like her, do you?" Emily said.

"I just don't want anyone taking advantage of you," Jake said.

"How could she take advantage of me?" Emily asked. "Why would you say that?"

Jake wanted to tell Emily how Melody was making fun of her behind her back, but he didn't want to upset her when she had tryouts the next day. He certainly didn't want to tell Emily the things Melody said about her. That would just hurt Emily's feelings. For now, all he could hope for was that Emily would make the cheering squad and Melody wouldn't. "It's nothing," he said. "Just a feeling."

"When you know Melody better you'll like her, too," said Emily.

She stood up. "See you tomorrow," she said. "Will you hang around for the tryout results?"

"I wouldn't miss it for the world," he said. He gave her a thumbs-up sign. "Go for it, Em," he said.

Emily smiled and waved the paper with the tryout tips. "Thanks," she said. She ran up the steps to call her friends.

Joan was in the kitchen preparing dinner with her father when the phone rang. He answered it and handed the receiver to her. It was Emily.

"I have a whole bunch of tryout tips for cheerleading," Emily told Joan.

Cheerleading! thought Joan with alarm. What if my father overhears us talking about cheering?

She moved over to the stove, which was as far from her father as the telephone cord would allow. Why couldn't her family have a portable phone like everyone else? With a portable phone she could have had this conversation in another room. Why did her parents have to be so anti anything new? Why did they have to be so different from everyone else's parents?

When Emily was reciting tip number three, Joan's father came over to the stove to check the rice. Joan moved over to the refrigerator.

"Isn't that a good one?" Emily asked.

"Terrific," agreed Joan, but she was hardly listening to Emily. She was too busy avoiding her father.

By tip number seven Joan had moved to the table and back to the refrigerator. Her father was going to become suspicious if she didn't stop dancing around the room. She had to get Emily off the phone.

"That's great, Emily," said Joan. "Thanks for calling."

"There's one more cheerleading tryout tip," Emily said.

"Oh, sorry," said Joan. "What is it?"

" 'Do your personal best,' " Emily told her, " 'and know that your best is the best you can do.' "

"Okay," said Joan. "I'll do that."

"You should feel very confident going out there tomorrow," Emily told her. "You'll make a great cheerleader." She shouted, "The new flyer for CMS! Yes!"

Joan automatically whispered into the receiver, "Sh-sh."

"What did you say?" Emily asked.

"I said 'Sh-hould.' Should I do my homework now or later?"

"I'm going to do mine now," Emily said. "So I can relax before I go to bed. The important thing is to put cheering out of your mind now. Okay?"

"Yeah," Joan agreed. "Thanks. 'Bye."

Joan hung up the receiver and went back to peeling onions for the stir-fry chicken.

"Who was that?" her father asked. "One of your new chums from the debate team?"

"Yes," answered Joan. "She's from the team." As she said it, Joan thought, I mean cheering team, not debate team. But she didn't say that to her father. Does that count as a lie? she wondered.

"So what's the subject of the first debate?" her father asked.

"Ah, we don't know for sure who is going to be on the team yet," Joan answered. "We'll find out tomorrow." She was trying so hard not to lie.

"You must be at least thinking of subjects, with all the meetings you've been having," he said.

"Yes, of course," Joan said nervously. "We're, we're talking a lot about the importance of winning. One side says that to win — at sports — is the most important thing. The other side is arguing that competition isn't the essence of sports. Something like that. It isn't quite defined yet. It's a little hard because we aren't sure who's going to be on the team. But we're practicing a lot."

"Competition and sports sounds like an insubstantial subject to me," he said. "Can't they think of anything besides sports in that school?"

"Guess not," Joan said. She went back to peeling onions. Lying to her parents was awful. But so was not being able to do what she wanted. She loved gymnastics. She wanted to be a cheerleader. Her parents just didn't understand anything that she liked. Jeans. Rock music. Hollywood movies. Public schools. Portable telephones. The list was endless. But now she knew that she definitely agreed with her parents on one thing. They hated lying. And so did she.

Tears streamed down Joan's face as she worked. She always cried when she peeled onions.

This time her weepy eyes were caused by more than the onions.

SEAVIEW TERRACE 6:30 P.M.

Alexis stretched out on her father's easy chair to watch a women's college basketball game on television. A good thing about being at her dad's was that the TV was hooked up to a satellite dish that pulled in great sports channels. She was watching a game between the University of Oregon and Stanford University. Oregon's number twelve was dribbling down the court. Alexis studied the dribble, noticing how far the player bent toward the ball. She'd try dribbling that way the next time she threw baskets with the kids at the playground.

The phone rang as number twelve threw the ball from midcourt. The ball arched through the air and swished down through the net.

"What a shot!" the excited announcer shouted as Alexis hit the mute button but kept her eye on the television screen. She picked up the phone and said hello.

"It's me," Emily told her. "I was so nervous about tryouts tomorrow that I made this list. It's things to help us do our best."

Alexis tried to watch the muted game while Emily read her list of tryout tips. The excitement she'd been feeling while watching the game was replaced by anxiety about the tryouts. What if she wasn't paying enough attention to Emily's suggestions? What if she didn't make the squad because she hadn't learned them?

Alexis turned her back on the TV and took the portable telephone to the dining table where she'd left her notebook. "Start over," Alexis said as she opened the pad to a clean page. "I'm going to write them down. I need all the help I can get."

When Alexis finished writing down Emily's tips, she looked back at the TV. There was only a three-point spread in the score, with Stanford in the lead. Alexis scanned the screen for number twelve. There she was, charging down the court and making another three-point basket! I'd love to be able to play like that, thought Alexis.

"Alexis," Emily said, "are you still there?"

Alexis turned her back on the basketball game again. "Yeah, I am," she said.

"It's going to be so much fun if we both make the squad," Emily said.

"There are a lot of kids trying out," Alexis reminded her. "And a lot of them are good. What if you make it and I don't?"

"It could be the other way around," said Emily. "You might make the squad and I won't."

"I don't want to be a cheerleader if you aren't," Alexis blurted out. She said it almost without thinking. But she knew when she heard herself that it was the truth.

"Alexis Lewis!" Emily exclaimed. "I wouldn't let you not be a cheerleader just because I wasn't."

"Well, it's not going to be a problem, since I'm not going to make the squad," said Alexis.

"No more negative thinking!" Emily scolded. "We've practiced a lot. Now we're both going out there to do our best. That's all we should be thinking about."

"You're right," Alexis agreed. "Do our best."

"But tonight we should put cheering out of our minds and relax," Emily advised. "Don't even practice tonight."

After Alexis hung up the phone, she turned the volume back on the TV, but she was still thinking about cheering.

If I don't make the squad and Emily does, thought Alexis, we'll hardly ever see each other. Emily will always be busy with practices or games. She'll be with her new friends — like

Joan and Melody — all the time. She'll never invite me over. It will be the end of our being best friends. I know it will.

A lump rose to her throat.

Tomorrow her life might change forever.

DOLPHIN COURT APARTMENTS 8:30 P.M.

Melody and her mother climbed the outside stairs to their apartment.

"I thoroughly enjoyed that meal," Carolyn Sinclair said. "But you barely ate yours, sugar."

"I told you," Melody said, "I'm not very hungry."

Carolyn opened the door, switched on the light, and they walked in. "With all the cheerleading you've been doing you should have a huge appetite," she said. She looked deep into her daughter's eyes as if she were trying to read her mind. Melody hated it when her mother did that.

"Melody, you're not on one of those crazy diets, are you?" she asked. "You're not trying to lose weight because you think it will increase your chances for making that squad?"

"No!" Melody answered. "I don't even care about that cheerleading stuff. I hope you didn't tell everyone in your office that I'm trying out."

Her mother broke the eye lock with Melody and looked around the room. Her gaze landed on the blinking answering machine. "There are some messages," she said. "Will you check them?"

Melody knew that her mother had changed the subject because she had blabbed at work about her daughter trying out for the CMS cheer squad. *Why did I have to be so enthusiastic about cheering after that first clinic?* Melody thought as she walked over to the answering machine. *I was such a fool. Why did I tell anyone that I was going out for it in the first place? Why did I e-mail my friends and dad in Miami all about it?*

It was all so embarrassing. Maybe she'd just skip school tomorrow. Be sick. Cut. Do anything but go out for cheering and make a fool of herself.

Melody hit the play button on the answering machine and listened.

"Hi, Melody, it's Sally. Just wishing you good luck tomorrow. Remember what I said and you'll be fine. Call me if you have any questions. 'Bye."

The next message was from Emily.

"Melody, it's me, Emily. Hi. Listen, I made up this list of tryout tips to help us get ready for the big day tomorrow. There are a lot of them, and I don't want to fill up your answering machine. So call me, okay? Then I can tell you about them. Also, I wanted to ask you something about . . . I mean . . . please call me. Okay?"

The next message was from her father.

"Check out tomorrow's tie. Oh, yeah, good luck with that cheering business tomorrow. You're the best. They'd be fools not to choose you."

Melody could hear the familiar sounds of the TV studio in the background. Her father had taken time out from his busy day to call her. Too bad she was going to disappoint him. Too bad she wasn't still in Miami. Whatever made her think she should go out for some stupid little cheer squad in Boremore? Forget cheering. Forget new friends. Forget tryout tips. She performed terribly at the clinic today, and she knew it. Even suggestions from Sally didn't help. Nothing was going to help her.

Melody went to her room, closed the door, put on some music, and took out her homework. She wouldn't go out for cheering. She'd be a loner in Boremore, get good grades, and wait it out until she could move back to Miami.

An hour later the phone rang. She didn't answer it. "It's for you, Melody," her mother shouted from her bedroom. "Pick up."

It was Emily. Enthusiastic, friendly Emily.

Melody didn't have the heart to tell Emily that she wasn't going to try out for cheering, so she listened to the tryout tips.

Emily began. " 'Concentrate on your own performance. Don't worry about what the other girls are doing.' "

Emily's first tryout tip totally contradicted Sally's advice about keeping an eye on the other cheerleaders.

Number four didn't make any sense either. " 'Exaggerate your moves. Make it SHARP!' " When I did that, Sally said the coach didn't like it, thought Melody.

And what about Emily's next tip? " 'Make jumps high, point toes, land light, SMILE.' " If I jump as high as I can, thought Melody, I might be higher than the other girls. According to Sally that's not good.

"Here's the last one," Emily continued. " 'Do your personal best, and know that your best is the best you can do.' In other words, don't hold back. Give it your all."

If I do my personal best, thought Melody, I'd be jumping high, landing soft, and making sharp movements. But that's what Sally said not to do.

"That's it." Emily was saying. "Those are my tryout tips. What do you think?"

"Great," Melody said. "Thanks, Emily. That was really sweet of you. Thanks for calling."

"Are you nervous?" Emily asked.

"Not really," Melody said. "I've been thinking I might not go out for cheering tomorrow. I don't like it as much as I thought I would."

"But you were so good. I mean you *are* so good. I mean . . . well, here's what I wanted to talk to you about. You were *great* the first two days. Then today, you didn't seem to be with it."

"I thought I was jumping too high," said Melody. "And I wasn't sticking my landings. My movements were too big. I was trying to improve all that today."

"I think it was much better when you were more relaxed and not thinking about all of those things," Emily told her. "Maybe I shouldn't have said anything, but you were so good before. I just think if you cheer at the tryouts the way you did the first two days, you'll have a great chance of making the squad."

"Thanks for telling me," Melody said.

"I want to help," said Emily.

"I know," said Melody. "Look, I have to go now." She said good-bye and hung up.

Melody sat on the edge of her bed and thought about Emily's phone call. Sally was telling her to cheer one way. Emily was telling her to cheer another way. Whose advice was she going to follow? Another seventh-grader going out for cheering or the best cheerleader on the squad? Wouldn't it make more sense to trust Sally?

She looked around her new room. Her eyes landed on a brown leather notebook on the middle shelf. She took the book off the shelf. Her grandmother had written the family history on the yellowed pages. Melody closed her eyes and flipped through the pages. When she stopped flipping, she put the tip of her index finger on the page and opened her eyes to see where it pointed. She read, "Whenever I don't know what to do next with my life, I remember what *my* mother told me. 'When you need advice, look to yourself. Trust your own heart and mind. Then, sugar, don't hold back. Live life to the fullest.' "

Melody read the passage again and gently closed the book. "Thank you, Grandma," she whispered. "And thank you, Great-Grandma."

Melody looked up and saw her own face in the mirror. Trust yourself, she thought. Don't hold back. Live life to the fullest.

Suddenly, she didn't care about Sally. She didn't care what anyone else thought about how she cheered, even the judges. She was going out for cheering tomorrow and doing it the best *she* knew how. She'd treat it like a dance performance, which meant she would give it her all and show her stuff.

Melody went to the kitchen to get a snack.

She was hungry after all.

GIRLS' LOCKER ROOM. FRIDAY 3:10 P.M.

Emily, Alexis, Joan, and Melody picked out lockers next to one another. The locker room was buzzing with nervous energy that went from girl to girl like an electric current.

Emily didn't know how she made it this far through the day without having a nervous breakdown. How was she supposed to keep her pretryout jitters under control when every seventh-grade girl who was trying out was as jittery as she was? It had been going on all day. In the hallways, as they went to and from classes, they exchanged glances that said, "Am I going to make it? Are you going to make it?"

As the tryout girls walked into the gym, Sally handed them each a sticker with a number on it. "Stick it to the upper left-hand side of your T-shirt," she instructed. "And good luck."

Emily was number four.

Alexis was number ten.

Melody was number thirteen.

And Joan was number twenty.

Four judges were seated at small tables set up for them in the four corners of the room. The girls lined up along the side wall. Melody counted twenty-eight girls, which meant that more girls had decided not to try out since yesterday's clinic. Should she have been one of them? Was she about to make a fool of herself?

Coach Cortes, who had been talking to one of the judges, came over to the cheerleading hopefuls and stood facing them. Instead of her usual shorts and T-shirt, she was dressed in a blue skirt, white blouse, and high heels.

"Tryouts are difficult," Coach told the girls. "For all of us. But especially for you. As you know, we only need ten girls to fill out the squad. That means eighteen of you are going to be disappointed today. Before we begin, I want to tell you how very impressed I've been with all of you over the last three days. You are a spirited, hardworking group. I hope that you will bring that spirit and attitude to whatever you do."

Emily tried slow breathing to keep her nerves under control. It wasn't working very well.

"Before I introduce our judges," Coach Cortes continued, "I'll remind you what you are to do for your tryout. When I call your number, you will perform for four separate judges. Look at the signs in the four sections of the room so you know what to do for each of the judges."

Emily looked and saw the four signs: RE-QUIRED CHEER. JUMPS. TUMBLING. DANCE.

"When you've finished all four tryout requirements, wait in the bleachers. No talking until the last girl has finished her last requirement. Then you will go back to the locker room to change. When you are ready, go to the front lobby, where our ninth-grade cheerleaders will serve snacks. After we've finished tallying the scores, I'll post an alphabetical list of the complete CMS cheer squad on the bulletin board to the right of the gym doors. If your name is on the list . . . well, you know what it means."

Melody's heart was beating like a drum. She wanted her name to be on that list.

Next, Coach Cortes introduced the judges — a high school cheerleading coach from Fort Myers, Florida, the Claymore High School coach, a representative from Cheer USA, and a retired college cheerleading coach.

Finally, Coach said, "Everybody take a deep breath, and let's begin."

The girls sucked in and let out their breaths in a collective swish. A few people, including Coach, laughed at the noise they'd made. Emily checked out the judges. Only one of them was smiling.

"So, are you ready?" Coach asked.

A few girls answered yes. Mostly they nodded silently.

"I said, are you ready?" Coach Cortes shouted.

"Yes!" the girls shouted back.

"Now have fun," Coach Cortes told them. "It's not a funeral."

Maybe not for you, thought Alexis.

Coach picked a small slip of paper from a bowl on the table, read it to herself, and announced, "The first to go is number ten."

Number ten, thought Alexis. That's me! She was frozen in terror.

Emily grabbed her hand and squeezed it. "Go," she whispered. "You can do it!"

Alexis took one last look at Emily before running out to the middle of the floor. How awful, she thought. I'm the first one to go. Her heart pounded. She started the chant. It sounded lonely and hollow. It was so scary to be cheering alone. Alexis thought about Emily's tips and smiled broadly. She tried to remember to have a positive, confident attitude. Smile, she ordered herself.

It was over. Alexis forced herself to flash the dance judge one last smile before leaving the floor. If you pick Emily, please pick me, too, she prayed. Please. She ran off the floor, relieved that it was over.

The sixth girl to try out was Joan.

Forget about your parents and what you'll do if you make the squad, she thought when she heard her number. Just go out there and do it!

As Joan was running to the required cheer corner, she felt light and happy and very excited. **"Give me a C,"** she shouted. Then she went to the jumping judge. Her jumps were high and light. Next, a few somersaults, three cartwheels, and two back handsprings for the tumbling judge. Last, the dance judge. That was fun. And she was done. Emily gave Joan a thumbs-up sign as she ran off the floor.

Five more girls tried out, and it still wasn't Emily's turn. Don't think about how good these other girls are, she told herself. Think about doing *your* best. Do it for CMS.

Finally it was Emily's turn. As she ran over to the required cheer judge, she imagined the bleachers were filled with fans at a basketball game. CMS was three points behind with only sixty seconds left on the clock. It was up to her to fire up the crowd and give the team the confidence they needed to win the game. **"Give me a C!"** she shouted.

Melody watched Emily do her four requirements. Melody was impressed with Emily. She was following her own advice and giving it her best shot. Melody remembered how in dance performances she loved the energy and excitement of going all out.

"Number thirteen," Coach called.

As Melody passed Emily coming off the floor, she heard her say, "Go for it." I will, thought Melody as she took her place in front of the judges and began the chant. She jumped as high as she wanted and landed as lightly as she did when she did ballet leaps. And since she knew how to do a back handspring, she threw that in at the end of her tumbling tryout. She did the dance routine with all her heart and soul and some of her ever-cool attitude.

After the last girl had tried out, they all went back to the locker room. Everyone was talking at once about what they thought they'd done wrong and how well the other girls had done. After they changed they went to the lobby to wait and wait.

And wait.

OUTSIDE GYM DOORS 5:30 P.M.

Finally Coach Cortes came through the gym doors with Sally and Mae. Coach was holding a rolled-up piece of paper. Sally held a small stack of envelopes.

A wave of girls moved toward the bulletin board. Coach Cortes called out, "Hold it. Stay back until I post the notice." They moved a few steps back. "Do not, I repeat, *do not* come up to the bulletin board until I am safely out of here."

Nervous laughter rose from the crowd.

"I have one announcement before I post the list. The CMS cheerleaders are invited to a dinner prepared and served by the football team at seven tomorrow night.

"You will have your first cheerleading meeting after the dinner and you'll be measured for uniforms." Coach looked over at Sally and asked, "What have I forgotten?"

"The parental permission slips," Sally told her. "They have to bring them to the dinner."

"Right," said Coach. "If you make the squad, we will give you a permission slip for your parents to sign. Don't leave here without one, and don't come to the dinner without bringing it back signed. Very important. Essential. Bring it."

A sudden chill ran through Joan's body. Goosebumps rose on her arms and legs. She wasn't just nervous anymore, she was terrified. If she made the squad, her parents had to sign a permission slip by tomorrow!

The lobby became absolutely quiet as Coach Cortes posted the cheer squad list. Emily held her breath.

Coach finally walked back into the gym. The doors closed behind her, and the wave of girls moved forward again. All Joan could see were backs. Suddenly she was in the air above the crowd. Emily, Melody, and Alexis were holding her up.

"Tell us, Joan," Emily yelled. "Who's on the list?"

Joan silently read the list from the top. "Emily! Emily!" she shouted. "You made it!"

Joan almost fell out of the lift as Emily shouted, "I made it. I made it!"

Joan put her hands on Emily's and Alexis's

heads for balance as she continued looking down the list.

"Who else?" asked Emily. "What about Alexis?"

"Oh! Oh!" Joan exclaimed. "I made it. Melody, you made it, too. You're on the squad!"

Melody felt a wave of excitement and happiness charge through her as she helped Joan out of the lift.

"I did it! I did it!" Melody shouted. "I made it!"

Joan and Emily were hugging her. They were all on the list. They were CMS cheerleaders.

Emily broke away from the hug and looked around. "Where's Alexis?" she asked.

The three friends looked at one another in alarm.

"She didn't make the squad!" Emily said with a sudden, terrible realization.

Emily ran over to the list and quickly went down the row of names to double-check. It was true. Alexis Lewis was not on the CMS cheer squad. Emily looked around the lobby. Disappointed, tearful would-be cheerleaders were leaving as quickly as possible. One girl was throwing up in the trash bin. So many people hadn't made the squad. They must all feel awful, thought Emily. And one of them is Alexis.

Emily ran out of the building without waiting for Joan and Melody. She had to find Alexis.

Joan took the permission slip from Sally and walked toward the exit in a daze. Maybe I can sign my parents' names to the slip, she thought. That will give me more time to tell them. But what about the special dinner tomorrow night? And the meeting? She was supposed to be proud and happy because she was chosen to be a CMS cheerleader, but here she was feeling miserable.

Joan walked outside. Where would she go now? What would she do? She saw her brother walking toward her. Jake Feder, on Rollerblades rolled beside him.

"We just heard you made the cheering squad," Jake said as he rolled around her. "Congratulations! That's awesome."

"My kid sister is a CMS cheerleader," Adam said. "I'm so impressed."

"You don't look very happy," Jake observed.

"I'm happy," Joan told him as she flashed the two boys a false smile. "Happy. See."

Adam gave her a surprised look. He knows I'm faking it, she thought.

"Who else made the squad?" Jake asked.

"Emily and Melody," Joan answered.

"Emily must be so psyched," said Jake.

"All the eighth-graders kept their spots on the squad," Joan said. "And the two other seventh-graders are Kelly and Maria. They were really good." Joan let herself enjoy the moment.

She was a CMS cheerleader!

OUTSIDE GYM DOORS 5:45 P.M.

Melody needed to get a permission slip from Sally, but she didn't know what to say to her. After all, she hadn't followed Sally's cheerleading advice. Why did Sally give me such bad advice? she wondered.

Finally, Melody went over to Sally.

"Congratulations," Sally said. "You were great out there today."

"Thanks," Melody replied.

"Don't mention it," said Sally. "I was glad to help. I know I really pushed you, but it worked."

"I sort of did the opposite of what you told me," Melody confessed. "When I tried what you told me I cheered badly."

Sally laughed. "That was the idea, Melody," she said. "I used some reverse psychology on you. It made you really think about cheering and what it's all about. You had to go through that to come out with the great performance you did today. If you had continued cheering the way you were, you never would have made the squad. Believe me."

"I see," Melody said, even though she wasn't

sure she really understood how Sally had helped her. But it didn't make any difference now. The important thing was that she was a CMS Bulldog cheerleader.

Melody and Sally left the school building together. When they came outside, Sally whispered to Melody, "Remember, don't tell anyone that I helped you make the squad. It will look like I was playing favorites."

"Okay," agreed Melody.

They saw Joan, Adam, and Jake and went over to them. Sally put an arm around Joan's shoulder. "Your little sister is amazing!" she told Adam. "You should have seen her out there. She'll be the best flyer CMS ever had."

Adam smiled at his sister and then returned his gaze to Sally. She gave him a big Sally smile.

"And you made it, too," Adam said, turning to Melody. "Congratulations."

"Thanks," Melody said. "I'm so excited. When I first moved here I was homesick for my friends in Miami, but then I met Emily, and she got me to go out for cheering. It's great."

Jake studied Melody. Maybe she had complained about Claymore to Sally because she was homesick. That was normal. And maybe she did call Emily "that chubette," but it was clear that she appreciated Emily. She wasn't faking it. Jake decided that if Emily could be Melody's friend, he could, too. But where was Emily? Jake looked around. "Where's Emily?" he asked.

"I think she went to look for Alexis," Melody told him. "Alexis just disappeared. She must be upset about not making the squad."

"Poor Alexis," said Jake.

"I feel awful that we all made the squad and she didn't," Melody said.

Jake looked into her eyes and knew that she wasn't pretending.

"I'm going home now," Melody told Adam and Joan. "I want to make some phone calls to see if I can find out what happened to Alexis. You going now?"

"Yeah," said Adam.

"I'll walk with you, then," Melody told them.

"Great," said Adam.

"I'll go partway with you," said Jake. "I want to hear all about the tryouts."

Sally noticed that Jake kept looking at Melody. How many guys does that girl need? she wondered.

"You go in the same direction, Sally," Melody said. "You want to walk with us?"

"I still have a few things to do here," Sally told her.

Sally kept her smile going as she said goodbye, but she was cursing to herself. Beautiful Melody Max had made the squad. Melody, who jumped higher than anyone, did a flip like she was made of air, and danced like she was on Broadway. Melody, who had the potential to outshine her.

Not in this lifetime, you won't, thought Sally.

SEAVIEW TERRACE 6:00 P.M.

Emily pressed the buzzer to Alexis's father's apartment. When no one answered the door, she sat on a deck chair and wrote Alexis a note. She'd leave it for her, then she'd go looking for Alexis on the beach. One way or another, she had to find her friend.

When she finished writing, Emily bent down to push the note under the door. A hand fell on her shoulder. She was startled and let out a little shriek of fright.

"Emily, it's just me," a low, sad voice said.

Emily stood up and faced Alexis. Her eyes were puffy and bloodshot from crying. She looked so sad that tears of sympathy sprang to Emily's eyes.

"I was just leaving you a note," Emily told her. She handed Alexis the piece of paper.

Alexis took the note and read it.

Alexis, I'm sorry you didn't make the squad and I did. Maybe you are upset because you think we won't be best friends if one of us is a cheerleader and the other isn't. But that isn't true. Would you stop being my friend if you had made the squad and I hadn't? We didn't stop being friends when you were on the basketball team and I wasn't. Can you come for dinner and a sleep over tonight? I'd be so happy if you would come. I can't be happy about being a cheerleader when you are unhappy. We have to find a way to make you happy, too. That's what friends are for. So please come over tonight. For me. Love always, your very best friend in the whole world, Emily.

"I don't want to ruin your happiness by being sad," Alexis told Emily. "It's just that I wanted to be a cheerleader, too. So we could do everything together in middle school."

"Were you going out for cheering because it was what I wanted to do?" asked Emily. "Sometimes I wondered if you even liked cheering that much."

"I didn't," Alexis admitted.

"That's good to know," Emily said with a sigh. "We still will do almost everything together, you know. Like tonight. Will you come to my house? Please."

"Okay," Alexis agreed. "Come on in. I'll call my dad and get my stuff."

Alexis knew that wanting to be with your

friends wasn't enough of a reason to be a cheer-leader. But while she packed her overnight bag, she still couldn't stop thinking about all the times she and Emily wouldn't be together, like all the out-of-town games and whenever Emily had practice. What will I be doing while Emily's busy with cheering? Alexis wondered. Maybe there was something else she could do after school at CMS.

Emily handed Alexis her hairbrush to pack. "What do you want to do after school?" she asked.

Alexis looked at her in amazement. "I was just wondering the same thing," she said. "You read my mind again."

"You're the only person in the whole world I can do that with," Emily told her. She smiled. "That's not going to change."

Alexis smiled back. "I know," she said softly.

"So that's what we have to think about," Emily said in a matter-of-fact tone. "We have to figure out what you do want to do. Okay?"

"Okay," Alexis agreed. "But tonight we're go-ing to celebrate that you made the squad."

"I did, didn't I?" Emily said with delight. She punched the air and shouted, "Yes!"

"Yes!" Alexis cheered. "And the squad is so lucky to have you."

"I just wish you were a cheerleader," Emily

said. Then Emily felt bad about what she said.

Alexis smiled at her best friend. "You know what?" Alexis told her. "I'm really sort of happy that I'm not a cheerleader. I hated all that smiling stuff and the shouting, too. I was dreading it."

"Congratulations on *not* being a cheerleader!" Emily told her.

"Thank you," Alexis said with a giggle.

The two friends broke out laughing.

HARBOR ROAD 6:15 P.M.

When Joan, Melody, Adam, and Jake reached Delhaven Drive, Jake said good-bye to the others. He wanted to swing by The Manor Hotel to see if Emily and Alexis were there.

When he'd gone, Melody asked Adam and Joan if they wanted to go to her place for a swim. "My mom's working late tonight, but I'm sure she won't mind," Melody said. "She's been wanting me to make friends here. She's going to be out of her mind when I tell her I made the squad. We could have a cookout by the pool."

"I don't think so," Joan said. "Dinner is already planned."

"It's my turn to cook with our father," Adam explained.

After they said good-bye to Melody, Adam asked Joan, "Do Mother and Father know that you went out for cheering?"

She shook her head no.

"I didn't think so," he said.

Joan burst into tears. Her brother put his arm around her shoulder. "It'll be okay," he said. "We just need a plan of action. It'll be okay."

"What do you mean, it will be okay?" said Joan as she pulled away from him.

"They won't keep you from being a cheerleader," he said. "We'll explain that it's important to you . . ."

"Just the way we explained that it was important for me to do gymnastics, and they made me drop out?" she asked. "Or how about when I wanted to go to that sleep-away camp for horseback riding, and they made me go to a math camp? How about that? Huh?" More tears came, but now they were angry tears. "They never say no to you, Adam," she shouted. "So of course you don't think it's a problem. Well, don't tell them I made the squad, because I'm not telling them." She shook the permission slip envelope in his face. "I'm forging their names on this permission slip, and I'm going to the dinner and meeting tomorrow, and I'm going to be a cheerleader. I'm going to keep on lying to them. And if you tell . . . if you tell, Adam Russo-Chazen, I am never, ever going to speak to you again."

Before Adam could say anything or stop her,

Joan ran up the street. She'd go in the back door and sneak up the stairs. Her father wouldn't even hear her. He'd be translating and listening to classical music and in another world that didn't include crying daughters and cheer squads and the problems of a kid like her.

BULLDOG CAFÉ 7:30 P.M.

Alexis and Emily were baby-sitting for Lily while Emily's parents worked in the hotel and restaurant. Jake was the café busboy for the dinner shift. When the girls were almost finished eating, Lynn came by on her way home from her high school cheerleading practice.

Lynn leaned over the café railing and congratulated Emily. "I heard you made the squad," she said. "I'm so proud of you. The family tradition continues." She patted Lily on the head. "You're next, pumpkin," she said.

"I'm not a pumpkin," Lily protested. "I'm a human bean."

"Human *being*," Lynn corrected. "Or maybe you are a string bean."

"I'm a human *bean*," Lily insisted.

"Like a Beanie Baby, I guess," Lynn whispered to Emily and Alexis.

"I'm not a baby," Lily grumbled.

"I'm sorry you didn't make it, Alexis," Lynn said.

"It's okay," Alexis told her. "I'm not that upset about it."

After Lynn left, Lily asked, "Lexis, how come you're not a cheerleader?"

"Because I didn't get picked," Alexis told her. "But I'm going to do something else at school."

"What you going to do, Lexis?" Lily asked.

Jake leaned over to put a basket of hot rolls in the middle of the table. Before Alexis could think up something to tell Lily, he said, "Alexis is going to work on the school paper."

"I am?" said Alexis in astonishment.

"I hope you will," Jake told her. "I didn't think of it before because you were so busy with the cheering. What do you say?"

"I say great," Alexis told him.

"Jake, that is perfect," Emily said. "She was editor of our elementary school paper. She practically wrote the whole paper herself."

"I know," Jake said. "I read a couple of the issues. You're a really good writer, Alexis, especially when you're writing about sports. How would you like to cover sports for me? I did it last year, but I can't do that and be editor, too."

"I love sports," Alexis told him. "That would be great!"

"Can you cover the dinner tomorrow night?" he asked.

"Yes!" Emily and Alexis said in unison.

"How come you talk together?" asked Lily.

"Because we're best friends," Alexis and Emily answered — together.

DELHAVEN DRIVE 10:00 P.M.

Joan sat at her desk and tried again to copy her mother's signature from the front of one of her college books. If only she could make it look like her mother had signed the permission slip, that would be one problem solved. But only one — and her problems seemed to be mounting fast. At dinner her parents had noticed that she was upset.

"Have you been crying?" her father asked when she sat down for dinner.

"No," she said. "I'm tired." She told herself that it was only a half lie, because even though she had been crying, she was tired.

"Why aren't you eating your meal, Joanie?" her mother asked. "You love roast chicken."

"I'm not that hungry," Joan answered.

"Why wouldn't you be hungry?" her father asked.

"Don't know," Joan answered.

Adam gave her a look that said, Here's a chance to tell them about cheering. She gave him a look back that said, No way.

In her room now, she practiced writing

Michelle Russo again. Even if she forged her mother's signature for the permission slip, how was she ever going to manage to attend all the practices and games? And what about the out-of-town games?

Someone knocked on her door. Joan quickly stuck the permission slip and the page of forged signatures in her geography book.

"Joanie, it's me," her father said through the door.

"What do you want?" Joan asked.

"Your mother and I would like to speak with you in the living room, please," he said.

Joan's heart started to pound harder than it had before the tryouts. What did they want? Had they guessed her secret? Had Adam told them?

"I'll be right there," she called back.

A minute later Joan was sitting on a chair facing her parents, who sat side by side on the couch. Two against one, thought Joan. It's not fair.

At first her parents just stared at her. Then her mother leaned over and whispered something into her father's ear.

Her father nodded. "Yes," he said. "I agree."

"Agree to what?" Joan asked. "If you're talking about me and I'm here, you shouldn't ignore me. That's rude."

Joan couldn't believe her own ears. She sounded like a bratty kid. That was inexcusable behavior in the Russo-Chazen household. She expected a long-winded scolding from her mother or father, but it didn't come.

Instead, her mother said, "Your father and I are concerned about you, Joanie."

"Why?" Joan asked. There was that bratty-sounding voice again! "I mean," she said in a calmer, softer tone, "I mean, why are you concerned about me?"

"Because you don't seem happy at your new school," her father said. "Adam adjusted so easily when he first went there. We falsely assumed that you would have the same experience."

"But obviously you are not," concluded her mother. "So we wondered what we might do to make a better learning environment for you. We thought that perhaps we could hire a tutor, to enrich your studies."

"We would also consider sending you away to a boarding school in New England this year instead of waiting until you are in high school," her father added.

Joan jumped to her feet. "I don't want to go away to boarding school," she shouted. "I *love* CMS. I *want* to go there."

"You love it!" her mother exclaimed. "Then

why have you been projecting so much unhappiness the past two days? Why did you not eat your dinner?"

"Because I want to be a cheerleader!" Joan told them. "And I'm afraid you won't let me."

Her parents looked at her in shock.

"A cheerleader?" Paul said.

"At sporting events?"

"Yes," Joan told them. "A cheerleader. I love it. I'm not like you. I like to exercise."

"We also enjoy exercise," her father protested. "We go for hikes and walks. But cheering! It's so . . . so . . ."

"So important to me," said Joan completing the sentence. "I want to be a cheerleader, and the squad wants me. Please, please give me permission to be a cheerleader."

"Doesn't that take up a lot of time?" her father asked.

"Not so much," Joan answered.

"What about your studies?" her mother asked. "Won't they suffer?"

"And will you have time for the debate club?" asked her father.

"I'd have plenty of time for studying and the debate club, too," Joan told them. "You have to keep your grades up, or they won't let you stay on the squad. I can manage my time really well, you always say that about me. If I don't get top grades, I'll quit all on my own. I promise."

"Cheering is pretty harmless," her mother told her father. "They just go out there and shout a little. And jump up and down."

"It's probably a peer thing," her father said.

"And cheerleading isn't dangerous like gymnastics," her mother added.

"She'll tire of it," her father concluded.

Joan looked from one parent to the other in amazement. It sounded like they were going to let her be a cheerleader! They thought cheering was just a lot of shouting for the team. Maybe it was like that when they went to middle school, thought Joan. And since they don't watch television or follow sports, they don't understand about the gymnastics and dancing and all the skill that's involved in being a cheerleader. And she wasn't about to tell them.

"Please, may I be a cheerleader at CMS?" Joan asked.

Her father looked at her mother. Her mother nodded. "Yes, of course you may," her father said.

Joan was on her feet again. "Then I need you to sign a permission slip. It's no big deal, just like when there's a class trip. Be right back."

She jumped up and ran out of the room, practically knocking over Adam, who was eavesdropping in the hall.

"Way to go," he whispered. "I was standing by in case you needed me."

"I do now," Joan told him. "Distract them while I have them sign the permission form. I don't want them to read it. They have no idea that it involves gymnastics."

"Sure," said Adam.

Adam went into the living room, and Joan continued up the stairs.

When she came back a minute later she could hear Adam in action. He was reciting Shakespeare's *Hamlet*, taking all the parts. Her parents loved it when Adam did that stuff like that. It was how he convinced them to let him join the drama club.

As Joan came into the living room, she checked to see which parent was more engrossed in the recitation. Her mother was absolutely captivated. Joan put the paper in front of her and slipped the pen in her hand.

"Just sign it," Joan whispered.

Her mother glanced down and quickly scribbled her name and went back to Adam's performance of *Hamlet*.

Her father grabbed Joan's shirtsleeve and pulled her down on the couch next to him. "Watch this, Joanie," he commanded.

Joan slipped the signed permission slip back

in her notebook and sat on the couch between her parents.

She held the notebook to her chest, leaned back, and smiled as she watched her brother complete his recitation of *Hamlet*.

THE MANOR HOTEL 10:30 P.M.

Emily lay across her bed and watched the moon glowing outside her window. A smile spread across her face. "I made it," she thought happily. "I made it."

Lynn rapped on her door and came in. She threw herself across the bed beside Emily and propped herself up on her elbow.

"Hey," said Lynn. "Penny for your thoughts."

"Nothing special," Emily said. "I'm just glad I made the squad."

"I hope it isn't hard on you at CMS," Lynn said.

Emily rolled over on her stomach and faced her sister. "What do you mean?" she asked.

"It's not like you have to do everything that I did," Lynn explained.

"I know," Emily told her. "I'm a cheerleader because I want to be. Not because you were one."

"Good," said Lynn. She sat up and smiled down at Emily. "By the way, I'm really proud of you. I can't wait to tell all my friends that you made the squad."

"Thanks," said Emily. "And thanks for helping me train."

When Lynn left the room, Emily thought about what her sister said. She knew that Lynn was right. One of the reasons she was a cheerleader was because Lynn had been one. She had wanted to do everything Lynn did for as long as she could remember. But it was hard to follow in her older sister's footsteps.

Especially when Lynn was so much better at everything than she was.

CMS. SATURDAY NIGHT 7:00 P.M.

Melody's mother gave Melody and Joan a ride to the school, so they came into the school building together.

They stopped at the cafeteria door and looked around before going in. A long table in the center of the room was covered with a blue tablecloth, gold stars, and napkins. Twists of blue, white, and gold crepe paper hung above the table. And there was Darryl Budd putting out salads. Melody heard the sounds of her favorite group, the Raves, playing. Joan breathed in the delicious smells of spaghetti sauce.

"This is so much fun," she whispered to Melody.

114

"Wait for us," a voice called out.

Melody and Joan turned to see Emily and Alexis coming toward them. Alexis had a camera slung around her neck, a pencil stuck behind her ear, and a reporter's notebook in her hand.

After they all hugged and said hello, Emily told them that Jake was there, too, helping the football players with the dinner.

"For my article, I'm going to ask all the new cheerleaders the same question," Alexis told them. " 'Why did you want to be a cheerleader?' I need your answer before I leave, which will be after the dinner. Okay?"

"I can tell you right now," Joan said. "I wanted to be a cheerleader because I love gymnastics and I love CMS. I am going to support my new school in any way I can."

After Alexis wrote Joan's answer in her notebook the four friends went into the cafeteria.

Sally saw Melody. Sally knew that she looked great in her blue slip dress. But Melody had on cool cargo pants. Where does she buy her clothes? Sally wondered.

Darryl walked over to Melody. "Cool music," Sally heard him say. "Jake told me you lent him the disc. What other groups do you like?"

Sally skipped eavesdropping on the rest of their conversation and went over to welcome

Joan and Emily. She'd take care of Melody's popularity later.

As Sally greeted the three girls, she wondered what Alexis was doing there.

Alexis saw the question in Sally's expression and explained that she was on the newspaper staff and was writing an article about the new cheerleaders and the dinner.

"Great," said Sally. But she was annoyed that this cute girl was going to be working on the paper with Jake. And Emily. Why did she make the squad? Other girls tried out who were at the same level as Emily. She probably got picked because her family is so involved in CMS sports. Sally wondered if Emily really would be a good cheerleader. If she wasn't, it could interfere with the squad's chances in the Cheer USA competitions.

One of the football players came by with a tray of little franks. Sally noticed that while Emily was eating one frank, she took two more with her free hand. Not a good sign.

"Emily's parents donated the spaghetti sauce," Alexis told Sally. "It's the one they use in the hotel restaurant."

"Smells good," said Sally. She looked over her shoulder. Darryl and Jake were both talking to Melody now. It was time to break up that little trio. She stepped up on a chair and onto an empty table. She clapped her hands, and everyone's eyes turned to her. That's more like it, Sally thought, as she flashed them her best smile. Then she announced that the cheerleaders wanted to thank the football team for preparing and serving them dinner.

"So," she shouted, **"let's hear it for the cooking Blue."**

All the cheerleaders picked up the chant, clapped their hands twice, and repeated **"Blue."** They used arm movements for the next lines:

**Let's hear it for the Blue XX Blue.
C, M, S, cook Bulldogs, cook!**

Emily loved the way Sally had substituted cook for fight in the chant. Sally is so clever, she thought. She has the best ideas and the best school spirit. Emily hoped she could be half as good a cheerleader as Sally. I'll make her my role model, Emily decided.

"Let's hear it again!" Sally shouted.

"C, M, S, cook Bulldogs, cook!" the cheerleaders hollered.

Sally did a toe-touch jump in her leap from the table to the floor. The football cooks and waiters applauded.

"Let's eat," Coach Cortes shouted.

The cheerleaders ran over to the table and sat down.

Melody sat between Sally and Alexis. Alexis put her narrow reporter's notebook next to her plate. She was here to work.

"I have my answer to your question," Melody told her. "I want to be a CMS cheerleader because cheering is a perfect way for me to be part of my new town and school. I love the school spirit at CMS, and I'm proud to be on the CMS cheer squad."

Alexis wrote it all down, then looked up and smiled at Melody. "Excellent," she said.

Darryl came over with two plates of spaghetti. Sally noticed that he served her before he served Melody. She winked at Darryl and picked up her fork.

After they all had ice cream and chocolate chip cookies, the coach announced that the cheerleaders should go to the gym for the first official meeting of the full squad. As the girls were leaving the table, the boys came over with their own heaping plates of spaghetti. It was their turn to eat.

"I have an idea for a photo for the newspaper," Alexis told Melody. "The new cheerleaders in front of the table where the football players are chowing down."

Melody helped Alexis organize the shot.

Alexis looked through the viewfinder at the six smiling new cheerleaders. In the background she saw guys eating stringy forkfuls of spaghetti. She couldn't wait to see her photo and article in the *Bulldog Edition*.

Joan didn't mind that her picture was going to be in the school paper. Her parents knew that she was a cheerleader, and they had signed the permission slip. She was safe as long as they didn't know what a cheerleader did, especially a flyer.

"Guys, keep eating," Alexis said. "Girls, smile!" She took four shots of the scene.

Melody was eager for the *Bulldog Edition* to come out, too. She wanted to send a copy to her father. Maybe he'd come see her cheer sometime. She hoped their squad would be in the Cheer USA state competitions. Her father and Miami friends would be very impressed by that.

After the photo shoot, the cheerleaders went to the small gym for their meeting. It was time for Alexis to leave. As she was walking toward the front door, Emily came running up to her. "I forgot to say good-bye," she told Alexis.

"That's okay," Alexis told her. "But you know what else you forgot? You didn't answer my question about why you wanted to be a cheerleader. I have everyone's answer but yours."

"I've wanted to be a cheerleader all my life," Emily said.

"Wait a minute," Alexis said. She took out her notebook and pencil. "Okay. Start over."

"I wanted to be a cheerleader all my life," Emily repeated. "And now I am a cheerleader." Her voice was charged with excitement. "I love CMS. I love cheering."

"Got it," said Alexis as she closed her notebook. Sounds of talking and laughter reached them from the small gym. "You better go back. You don't want to miss the meeting."

Alexis watched Emily running happily back to the gym. I spent the whole summer dreaming about being a cheerleader with Emily, she thought. But somehow she felt all right.

She was going to be the best *Bulldog Edition* reporter.

DOLPHIN COURT APARTMENTS 11:00 P.M.

Melody Max turned on her computer and checked her e-mail. There were messages from three of her friends in Miami and one from her father. They all wanted to know how she did in the tryouts. She'd already called her dad with the good news. Now she'd write to her friends.

> Hey, out there, it's me — Melody Max, CMS
> cheerleader. Yes, I made it! Wow! For a while
> there I didn't think I could cut it. It's been a
> super stress scene over here on the west

coast. But with the help of some other seventh-graders, I pulled it out. Cheer tryouts are a who's-going-to-win-you-or-me kind of scene, but you know what? People were still helping one another. Wild, huh? No time to be bored anymore, so I think I'll be okay. Take that back. I KNOW I'm going to be okay. Did I whine a lot the first two weeks I was here? Sorry about that. Now I'm back on track. Still missing you all, but it doesn't feel like prison no more no how. Cheers! And love. The Max.

Melody sent her e-mail, switched off her computer and stared at the blank screen. She was tired and she suddenly felt very sad. Everything she'd said in the e-mail was true. She was excited about being a cheerleader, but she missed being with friends she'd known all her life. Like Tina. She and Tina thought they were so lucky to be best friends and live on the same block. Now Tina was on the other side of the state. Not so lucky. And her dad! She missed her dad so much it made her heart ache.

Melody got into bed and turned off the light.

THE MANOR HOTEL 11:15 P.M.

Emily had been in bed for an hour and was still wide awake. She turned her head on the pillow and faced her bedside table. She took a deep breath and smelled the delicate scent of the bouquet of white tea roses. The flowers, in a blue vase, were there when she came home. A note leaning against the vase read: *"Carry on the tradition! We're so proud of you. Love, Mom and Lynn."*

I'm so happy that I'm a cheerleader, Emily thought. It's my dream come true. She loved how her family was happy for her. And her friends — even Alexis who hadn't made the squad. But what about the people who thought she didn't deserve to be on the squad?

Emily rolled over onto her back and stared up at the ceiling.

She couldn't get the scene out of her mind. She was coming back into the gym after saying good-bye to Alexis when she thought she heard her name being called. She looked to her right and saw Kelly, Maria, and Sally talking together. "Well, the Grangers are a big-deal family in town," she overheard Sally say. "So of course they had to pick her." Emily walked quickly to the other side of the gym before they saw her.

Tears sprang to Emily's eyes and spilled out onto her pillow case. That's what she was afraid people would think if she made the squad.

Is Sally right? Emily wondered. Did I only

make the squad because of my family connections?

SEAVIEW TERRACE 11:25 P.M.

Alexis lay in bed thinking about her sports column. She wondered if Jake had given her the assignment because he felt sorry for her. What if her piece wasn't good enough? It would be so hard for Jake to tell her that. But he'd have to. That was his job as editor. All I can do is my best, she thought. Then she remembered that was what she had said to herself about cheering. She had done her best at cheering, but it wasn't good enough for her to make the squad. Would her best reporting be good enough for the *Bulldog Edition*?

The phone rang. It's Emily, thought Alexis. She's back home from the cheerleading meeting and wants to tell me about it. Alexis smiled to herself. She loved how she almost always knew when it was Emily calling her. Best friends, she thought. It's like we have mental telepathy. Maybe we do.

She reached over and picked up the phone on her desk. "How'd it go?" she asked.

"How did what go?" asked the person on the other end. It was her mother.

"I thought you were Emily," Alexis explained.

She tried not to sound too disappointed. But she was.

"I just called to say good night," her mother said. "I thought you might be alone like me."

"Dad's here," Alexis told her mother. "He's watching television."

"I figured he'd be out," said her mother, "since it's Saturday night."

"Well he's not," Alexis said.

She hated how her mother felt sorry for herself because her ex-husband had lots of dates and she didn't. Why does she have to tell me about it? Alexis wondered.

After she said goodnight to her mother she lay back on her pillow. Emily hadn't called her.

Was she losing her special connection with her best friend?

DELHAVEN DRIVE 11:30 P.M.

Joan had on her pajamas and was lying in bed, but she wasn't ready to fall asleep. There was so much to think about. She played the last two days over and over again in her mind like a favorite movie. She'd made the squad, her parents signed the permission slip, she'd been to a big dinner party at school, and attended her first cheerleader's meeting. She was even measured for her uniform.

The meeting was so great. Coach congratulated the eighth-graders on making it back on the squad and welcomed the seventh-grade cheerleaders. Sally and Mae passed out a schedule of the football games and cheerleading practices. The first game that the cheerleaders would cheer for was the big game between the Bulldogs and the Santa Rosa Cougars.

"We want to look very good at that game, girls," Coach had said. "You're all going to have to work extra hard, especially the new girls."

Joan closed her eyes and imagined herself cheering for CMS at the Bulldog/Cougar football game. She couldn't wait.

Tryouts were just the beginning.

ABOUT THE AUTHOR

Jeanne Betancourt has written many novels for young adults, several of which have won Childrens' Choice awards. She also writes the popular Pony Pal series for younger readers.

Jeanne lives in New York City and Sharon, Connecticut, with her husband, two cats, and a dog. Her hobbies include drawing, painting, hiking, swimming, and tap dancing. Like the girls in CHEER USA, she was a cheerleader in middle school.

Look for Jeanne Betancourt's next book in the **CHEER USA** series:

#2 Fight, Bulldogs, Fight!